MURDER ON A COUNTRY LANE

Gripping cozy English mystery fiction

JON HARRIS

Published by The Book Folks

London, 2023

ISBN 978-1-80462-124-0

www.thebookfolks.com

MURDER ON A COUNTRY LANE is the first novel in an addictive series of cozy English mysteries. Head to the back of this book for details about the other titles.

For my sisters

Chapter 1

All seemed perfectly at peace in the Barley Mow. Only the sound of the distant church bells striking a quarter to twelve disturbed the silence as the pub awaited its next customer. In short, there was nothing to tell of the murder that was about to shake the little village of Biddle Rhyne.

Julia watched from behind the bar as the door opened and a gust of autumn wind blew in followed shortly by the major.

The man made a noise reminiscent of a horse whinnying to emphasize how cold it was outside before taking off his overcoat and hanging it on one of the spare hooks by the door.

The major was a tall man and had to stoop slightly to get under the low oak beams as he crossed the parlour to the bar. He'd made the journey so many times that the bob and weave of it were second nature to him and if needed to, he could do it with his eyes shut. Or, as was more often the case, when too inebriated to properly see.

He reached the bar and put his hands solidly on the countertop before quickly withdrawing them as his fingertips landed in a wide puddle of cider that Julia had produced when pouring the previous order. He wiped them lightly on the front of his trousers.

Julia felt the man's eyes skim over her, taking in her dark features and slight frame, which looked even slighter in the fitted black shirt that the pub provided for her.

"You're not the usual girl," the major remarked, in his low, gravelly voice.

"You're right, I'm not," Julia replied. She forced herself to put on her best customer-service smile. It came with some difficulty; the shift had barely begun and already her feet were killing her. "Sally's off on her holiday so I've been covering her shifts this week."

"Hm, I see." The major removed his flat cap, revealing his bald dome, and placed the hat on the bar, taking care to avoid the pool of cider. "Well, a pint of best bitter then, please."

Julia dutifully pulled the drink. Well, the retired major obviously didn't recognize her, but she knew him well enough to know that he preferred the 'old man' style of glass with the dimples and the handle.

The major handed the exact cash over the bar – contactless obviously hadn't quite caught up to the man yet, despite him only being in his sixties – and took a long swig of the drink. When he moved the glass away, there was a thick tideline of foam left on his salt-and-pepper broomstick moustache. He smacked his lips together in satisfaction.

"Cheers, Sally," he said, automatically, as he turned away and headed towards his customary table next to the log fire where his broadsheet newspaper already lay waiting for him.

The door opened again and a grey tide of pensioners swept in. Julia had known they were coming; the Abbot's Mead care home had booked the whole dining room out for Sunday lunch. But somehow it took her aback to see the whole coachload of the village's most distinguished residents file past, mostly with the aid of walking sticks or Zimmer frames.

It seemed that no sooner had the dining room door closed behind them than the drink orders started coming, and kept coming. Barry, the pub's waiter, brought the orders in and took the trays of drinks away with his typical lack of urgency.

When the initial round of drinks was all poured and collected, there was a calm after the storm. Not that the old duffer had noticed, but the major's pint had been more foam than beer and Julia knew that barrel was going to need changing. Looking at the empty bar, now seemed as good a time as any.

Julia nudged open the door behind her and found Barry lounging idly in the staff corridor, as she had expected to.

"Watch the bar for two minutes, would you? I need to change a barrel," she said, beckoning him over.

Barry unpeeled himself from the wall and came over.

"Just make it quick, I'm due a cigarette break," he said, folding his arms and leaning on the bar.

Julia called him a name but only once she was safely halfway down the corridor towards the cellar.

When she returned, sweating and puffing, Barry was still exactly where she'd left him, arms folded on the bar.

He sighed as he straightened up. "You took your time."

"I was five minutes, tops," Julia said.

"More like twenty," Barry replied, heading back towards the staff corridor. "I'm going on my break now."

"Did you serve anyone?" Julia called after him, acutely aware of how unlikely it was that he'd have rung it through the till correctly.

"Nah, it's been dead," Barry said as he disappeared down the corridor.

A harrumphing noise behind her made Julia turn back to the bar. "Sorry! Hello, Major."

The major shot his head left and right before leaning in conspiratorially, in the process drawing far more attention to himself than he otherwise would have. When he spoke it was, by the major's standards, a low whisper. But by the standards of anyone without a prescription hearing aid that they refused to wear, it was reasonably loud. "Another pint of best, please, my girl."

Julia's hand was just beginning to reach towards the pint glass when a voice behind her made her stop.

It was Ivan, the Barley Mow's beleaguered landlord, who would spend the whole of the pub's opening hours rushing from room to room and down into the cellar and back, his enormous beer belly swaying back and forth as he went. He raised his voice at the major, whether out of irritation or just because of the major's deaf ears, Julia wasn't sure; his voice was thick with the local West Country accent.

"You need to give us your car keys if you want a second pint, Major, you know the rule."

Ivan didn't wait for a reply before bustling off through the door behind the bar. Julia felt a warm draft from the kitchens and briefly heard Ivan berating the waiter again for something before the door swung itself shut.

The major at least had the good grace to look sheepish. "There was an, er, incident a little while back involving my last car and, er, the duck pond outside the village hall," he muttered.

Julia suppressed a smirk. She did, of course, remember. As did everyone else in Biddle Rhyne. Goodness knows there was little enough going on most of the time. When a retired member of His Majesty's forces made an aquatic landing in the local duck pond it tended to make something of a splash.

"Now Ivan insists I hand my keys over behind the bar if I'm having more than just the one," the major continued, bitterly.

Julia nodded politely. The major just stood there, looking at her with puppy-dog eyes. She realized that he was trying it on; seeing if the new girl would let him avoid the ritual humiliation of handing over his car keys. She kept her features placid and waited. Julia felt that she was good at not doing things. It was how she seemed to spend most of her time these days.

Eventually the major turned away, mumbling something under his breath, and stomped back across the flagstone floor to where his coat hung and began rummaging through its pockets. He looked up from his search with his eyes wide.

"The bally things are gone!" he announced.

"I'm sorry, Major," Julia replied in a sing-song voice. "Ivan's word is law around here. I can't let you have another without them."

"Dash and blast it, girl, did you not hear me? I said my car keys are missing. I have bigger worries than a ruddy pint of beer."

Julia, slightly taken aback by the tirade, thought for a few moments. "Maybe you left them in the ignition?" she suggested.

The major scowled at her, but this quickly melted away. "Yes, well, best check, I suppose," the man said. He lifted the little latch on the door and stepped back out into the cold, pulling the door firmly behind him.

No longer able to maintain her mirth, Julia allowed herself to break into a fit of giggles. However this was quickly curtailed as Barry returned with yet another drinks order. Julia began filling glasses as Barry rather begrudgingly took the current tray of drinks and headed for the diners.

The front door slammed open and a voice echoed out across the room, making Julia lose track of how many Diet Cokes she had poured and how many regular ones.

"Gone!" the voice announced.

Julia rolled her eyes but didn't look up. "I know the car keys are gone, Major."

"Not my keys, my bally car is gone!" The major stormed over to the bar, his face red and his nostrils flaring, revealing an abundance of nasal hair.

"Really?" Julia asked.

"Of course, really. It's not where I parked it. Do you think I'm some kind of fool?"

Julia kept her thoughts to herself.

The major swore creatively. "Some beggars have gone and stolen the thing. And it's only a year old, too!"

Julia put down the last of the Cokes. In all honesty she didn't care if one of the pensioners in the next room got regular rather than diet.

"I'd better call the police," she said.

Chapter 2

A little mist of rain came down, just enough to make Julia turn on the wipers. Although mostly what they shifted was the continual fall of slimy yellow and orange leaves that tumbled from the sky. They weren't even near any trees. Where did they come from? It was a mystery to Julia.

In the passenger seat next to her, the major sat, breathing heavily through his nose and scowling out at the passing country lanes.

She didn't blame him for being in a dark mood. The police had said they wouldn't be able to send anybody out to investigate the car theft until that evening. After a very long and detailed speech on the state of the country – ruddy – and where it had gone – the dogs – Julia had offered to drive him home when her shift finished at three. The major had spent the first part of the afternoon getting sullenly drunk at his table while occasionally swearing at something he read in the paper.

The car protested as Julia tried to coax it up Pagan's Hill and the downshift into second was accompanied by its usual grinding sound that she promised herself she would get looked at as soon as she had a steady paycheque coming in.

As she turned a corner, a large 4x4 came barrelling down the other way, showing no intention at all of slowing, and forcing Julia to swerve to a halt in the mud-clogged entrance to one of the fields. She muttered a few opinions under her breath about the other driver's fitness to hold a licence as well as their penis size, despite the fact she hadn't caught a glimpse of them and had no idea of their gender.

Julia managed to get her car moving uphill again, more through force of will than anything she did with the pedals, which seemed entirely disconnected to how the engine behaved as far as she could tell. Although she'd lived in the village for the last ten years, almost half her life, she'd never been comfortable driving these country lanes which usually had either thick hedges or deep rhynes of water bounding their narrow curves in. To her continuing bafflement, none of the other locals seemed to consider them at all hazardous.

She'd just got back into second gear when the major suddenly sat bolt upright in his seat and pointed across the road, his arm shooting out across Julia and almost entirely obscuring her view of the road.

"That's my car," the major said, his finger jabbing repeatedly at the driver's side window.

Julia slammed on the brakes. She squinted in the direction the major was pointing. She found herself looking up Forge Lane, an even smaller byway than the one she was currently on, barely wide enough for a single car to squeeze down.

But squeeze down it a car had. Julia could see the rear section of a Jaguar sticking out from around the sharp bend.

"They'd better not have crashed it, the rogues," the major hissed as he flung the passenger door open and slammed it behind him.

Julia scrambled to get out and chase after the major. His long strides were difficult to keep up with, even if he was lurching a bit from side to side.

She couldn't help but guess that the front half of the car, hidden round the curve of the lane, had probably clipped the stone wall that she knew from recent experience was hidden in the hedgerow there.

The major reached the bend in the road before her and, after seeing the rest of his car, he turned to Julia, the colour draining rapidly from his face. He held a palm out towards her. "Don't look, my girl," he croaked.

Julia ignored him. *That man must be really fond of his car.* She rounded the bend herself and instantly wished she'd listened to the major. She only caught a glimpse before quickly turning away from the horrible scene, but it was more than enough for her. The car had indeed hit the stone wall, but pinned between the car and the wall was a person. Or rather their mortal remains. The body was as twisted and misshapen as the front of the car was.

* * *

The detective inspector scribbled something else into his notebook and carried on surveying the scene of the crash. The small group of paramedics stood idly by; there had been little they'd been able to do. Julia watched all of this from behind the hastily erected line of police tape that now cordoned Forge Lane off from the steep ascent of Pagan's Hill.

The rain was coming down faster now and she took shelter underneath the little fold-out umbrella which she always kept in her handbag. The major stood next to her as upright as a beanpole. He'd turned down her offer of sharing the umbrella and had only his flat cap to keep the rain off. Rivulets of water were now streaming off from it onto his coat, but he seemed unfazed.

"Nasty business," he said, once again.

Julia could only nod her agreement.

The detective flipped his notebook shut and made his way towards them, ducking underneath the police tape. He was a broad man, his size exaggerated slightly by the ill-fitting clothes that he wore: a long beige coat over a dark suit. He had a dark five o'clock shadow covering his jowls and a bushy moustache that had taken residence above his protruding lips. He gave a nod and spoke with a gentle Welsh lilt. "I think we've got everything we need here."

"What are your chances of catching them?" Julia asked him. "The driver, I mean."

The DI gave a non-committal shrug. "Fairly decent, I'd say. Often with a hit-and-run someone comes forward once they've cooled off and it all sinks in. If not, I can start questioning the usual teenage troublemakers in the village and their parents. See who has an alibi and who hasn't. It should whittle the list down pretty quick."

He turned to the major. "I know you've identified Mrs Audrey White, but we might need you to come down to the morgue to make a formal identification tomorrow."

"Right you are, Constable," the major said.

Julia caught the DI wince at the incorrect title. "Did you say Mrs White?" she asked.

"Yes," the policeman replied. "Sorry, did you know her?"

"Not well. But everyone knew Mrs White. I don't think she was the most popular person in Biddle."

The major muttered something about speaking ill of the dead.

"I mean," Julia persisted, "have you considered the possibility that this might have been deliberate? I could name offhand a couple of people who bore Mrs White a grudge."

The DI gave a heavy sigh. "Look, I think maybe you've been watching too much TV. These lanes are a magnet for speeding motorists. And there's a reason it's a crime, even if the vehicle isn't stolen. It's dangerous. And this, regrettably, can be the consequence." He flapped an arm in the direction of the crash.

Julia inwardly recoiled at the accusation that she watched too much TV. She only ever watched the news and *Bake Off*. It was then that Julia realized that she recognized the copper. DI Jones. Rhys to his friends, which she wasn't.

She knew him from last year when she used to work behind the bar at the rugby club. He was there like clockwork anytime Wales were playing. She seemed to recall that they had a match this afternoon and wondered if that had anything to do with his keenness to be done for the day.

Julia stared at the policeman as the rain drummed down onto her umbrella. She fought a brief but vicious internal struggle. On the one hand, she could tell Jones about the death threat she'd found a week earlier. But on the other hand, she'd then have to explain why she was snooping around in the locked drawers of Mrs White's office.

"I'm just saying, maybe it's worth looking into," Julia said.

"And I'm the professional here and I'm saying it's not. So why not get yourself back home under a blanket with your kitten or whatever you do with your evenings and leave this in hands that are a little less manicured and a little more capable."

With that, Jones turned his back and strode away to where his car was parked next to the police line. Julia scowled into his back. He obviously didn't know her at all. She was a dog person, not a cat person, and it would be a puppy keeping her company under the blanket.

"What a fat head," the major said.

"I couldn't have put it better myself."

"Still, he's probably right; these lanes were an accident waiting to happen. All the bally time I find cars careening down here at what seems like ninety miles an hour, some spotty youth behind the wheel. Er, no offence."

Julia hadn't realized that she was counted among the ranks of the spotty youths. Better than being retired with one foot already in the grave, she supposed.

"Come on, let's get you home," she said, clicking the little mechanism to collapse her umbrella down and turning towards her car. "I promise I'll drive carefully."

The major gave a deep sigh before he followed her. "What a ruddy awful business," he said again. "Barely ten thousand miles on the clock and she's completely written off."

Julia shook her head as she turned the key in the ignition and then waited while Jones's large grey sedan made a belaboured three-point turn around the narrow confines of the lane. She noticed that his wing mirror snagged the police tape as he finally completed the manoeuvre and pulled it from its fixtures, leaving it to stream away in the gusty wind. What an incompetent fool of a policeman. She was going to have to do some investigating of her own.

Chapter 3

Julia pulled up alongside the house and threw the car into reverse gear. She gave it a good bit of wellie to get up the steep driveway but despite the bellow of the 0.8l engine the car remained perfectly still.

She sighed, put it back into neutral and then into reverse again, making sure that the gears connected this time. She successfully managed to guide the car between the narrow gateposts and up the driveway. The parking sensors, as was tradition, declined to switch on, so she stopped the car when she felt the gentle crunch of her rear bumper meeting the plant pots that protected the front of the house.

She slipped from the car and made a dash through the pelting rain, hopping nimbly over the puddle that formed by the front door, and with a quick fumble of keys she was inside.

There was a person standing just inside the doorway and Julia let out an ear-splitting scream of terror.

"Well, it's nice to see you too, cow," Sally said.

Julia touched her chest as she felt her heart rate gradually returning from about-to-be-murdered back to normal. "You're back from holiday early," she said. Her housemate hadn't been due home until the evening.

"No, you're back from work late," Sally replied. "Oh, my God, I have so much to tell you, I missed you! Now come here." With that, Sally enveloped her friend into a hug, but only with one arm because the other was holding a large, full glass of red wine safely at arm's length and out of harm's way.

Julia eyed the beverage once she was disentangled from the hug. "You didn't waste any time."

Sally's face lit up into a broad grin. "I figure that I'm still on holiday until tomorrow. Do you want one?"

"After the day I've had, I think I need one," Julia replied.

"What's wrong, chicken?" Sally asked.

"I just found Mrs White dead."

"Christ on a bike, really?"

Julia nodded. "Hit by a car. The police are treating it like a hit-and-run, but…" She trailed off.

"That note you found," Sally finished her thought off for her, as she so often did. "You don't think it might have been… murder, do you?" She finished in hushed tones, as though afraid to voice the words aloud.

"I don't know. I mean, it could be, right? It's a bit of a coincidence if someone threatened to kill her and then a week later…"

"Did you tell the police about the note?" Sally asked.

"What? And explain why my fingerprints were all over it? No, I'd prefer not to, thanks. I did point out that Mrs White wasn't exactly popular in the village but they still want to treat it as a hit-and-run."

Sally considered this for a moment and then reached out and took hold of her friend's hand. "Come on, let's get you that drink," she said. And with that she turned, flicking her long blonde curls out behind her, and led Julia towards the kitchen and, more precisely, the Haut-Médoc that sat open on the counter.

As the wine went down, Julia related the harrowing events of the day: the major's car being stolen, driving him home, finding Mrs White, and the blood-boiling incompetence of the local constabulary.

When Julia was done, Sally paused to take it all in and began fumbling with the gas fire mounted on the wall. Rumpkin, well attuned to the sound, appeared from wherever he'd been lurking and padded past Julia's chair to the warmth of the fire. Julia held her fingers out as he passed and let him stroke himself as he went by. She was just about to reach around the back of the chair for the comfort of the large woollen blanket that nestled there, when DI Jones's contemptuous words floated back to her and she stopped. It wasn't that cold, anyway.

"And you still don't know who wrote that note?" Sally asked, as she twiddled the fire to the exact setting she wanted and then sank down cross-legged in front of it, absent-mindedly stroking Rumpkin's hairy brown flank.

"Plenty of guesses. Unsubstantiated ones. But, no, not really," Julia said.

There was no shortage of people who would wish ill upon Mrs White. She owned – or *had* owned, Julia mentally corrected herself – the small garden centre on the edge of the village, Only Gardens. By all accounts, she was not a very pleasant person to work for.

And then of course there was Lance Teller, the strapping thirty-something man who crafted artisan pots in his workshop. It was common knowledge that every Sunday, when Janice Teller went to church, Mrs White would slip off down the footpath to the Tellers' cottage and spend Sunday morning performing less than holy acts with Lance. No surprise, then, that Only Gardens decided to stock a wide range of Lance's pottery. The earthenware order wasn't the only thing he was fulfilling for the garden centre.

Julia shivered and instinctively reached up for the blanket and wrapped herself in it. That must have been what Mrs White was doing when she was hit by the car, she realized. The footpath between Mrs White's house and the Tellers' cottage ran right across Forge Lane. She must have been on her way back from her illicit engagement when she was run down.

Sally swilled the wine around in her glass, though it was mostly empty by this point, and contemplated the liquid as it sloshed round. She spoke thoughtfully as she watched it. "If the person who wrote the note did make good on their promise, then it narrows the list of suspects down, doesn't it?"

"How do you mean?" Julia asked. "Half the employees at the garden centre wanted to throttle the woman from what I gathered. Any one of them could have written that note."

"Right, right." Sally hauled herself up and made her way over to the sofa. The dog woofed softly in protest as she went. "But how many of them would have had the opportunity to steal the major's car?"

Julia sat upright. Now there was a thought. "None," she said. "The Barley Mow's dining room had been booked out by the care home. They were all eighty-year-old geriatrics who were dropped off by coach at the start and collected at the end. I can't see any of them being able to drive a car, let alone nick one."

Sally steepled her fingers together and planted her chin atop them. "You said the car keys were lifted from inside the pub, so who did have a chance to steal them? You did, I suppose." She looked at Julia over her fingertips.

Julia ignored the joke. "Staff, though. There's Barry."

"Disgruntled ex-garden centre employee." Sally nodded.

"And now working at the illustrious Barley Mow. Only with substantially decreased wages, no doubt." For all of Mrs White's many faults, she did at least pay her staff well.

"Would he have the chance to steal the car? I mean, he was working all day, wasn't he?"

"He did go out for a fag break. A long fag break," Julia added pointedly. "I heard Ivan giving him grief for it."

"How long, exactly?" Sally asked.

Julia thought for a moment, casting her mind back. "It can't have been more than twenty minutes. Well, not much more."

"Would that be long enough?"

"It would be stretching it. Maybe we can check, see how quickly we can walk from Forge Lane to the pub? The drive in the other direction would only be a couple of minutes."

"Right, that's tomorrow's job then," Sally said, evidently warming to the role of amateur sleuth. "Who else?"

"The kitchen staff, but there's no chance that Ivan would let them have more than about two minutes away during Sunday lunch without him raising bloody murder about it. And Ivan, of course. I doubt he left the pub while it was doing business, though, I think the whole place would crumble at the foundations if he did that. But I'll text the kitchen staff and double check."

With that, Julia shuffled under the blanket to get her phone out of her pocket and began to type.

"Janice Teller is the obvious suspect, of course," Sally said.

"Yes, the woman spurned," Julia said. "Even if she didn't take the keys then maybe someone could have swiped them and given them to her. I should probably text the vicar and make sure that Janice was at church this morning."

"You have the vicar's number, do you?" Sally asked with a frown.

Julia laughed. "No, I haven't had a sudden spiritual epiphany while you've been on hols. I can get it off the church website, though."

"And anyone else?" Sally prompted, when Julia put her phone back down.

"There was one man," Julia said. "A stranger, I didn't recognize him. He didn't do much, just sat in the parlour most of the day drinking lager. He did pop out a few times, I assumed for a fag. I didn't pay him much attention at the time. I can't think what he could have had against Mrs White, though, I'm sure I'd have known him if he was from around here."

Sally shrugged. "Keep your eyes peeled for him, I guess. What did he look like?"

Julia tried to conjure an image of the man. He hadn't made much of an impression at the time, but then again, why would he? "He had gingery-red hair and a moustache. Fifties, maybe sixties."

Over the next few minutes, as more wine went down and Rumpkin snored away happily to himself, Julia's phone chimed softly several times.

It transpired that Ivan had been almost omnipresent in the kitchen, being his usual perfectionist self and overseeing the roast dinners. And the vicar, somewhat puzzled, replied to say that Janice Teller had indeed been in attendance that day.

"It's not looking good for Barry, is it?" Sally mulled to herself as she emptied the last of her wine glass and reached over for the bottle that sat on the little side table between her and Julia.

* * *

Julia was sitting in the chair, hand dangling idly over the side where it rested on top of Rumpkin's head, and the gas fire flickered away to itself with a low purr. *Northanger Abbey* lay open on the arm of the chair, but this evening she wasn't able to concentrate.

It was only a small house; the front door opened straight into the living room and the staircase started right by the door, to the extent that you had to be careful opening it in case you clonked an unfortunate person just coming down the stairs. Julia had never quite forgiven Sally for that one.

The open arrangement meant that even with the fire on, it was difficult to keep the place warm once autumn drew in, but Julia had found that she didn't mind. Through a strategic use of blankets and hot-water bottles and, if things got dire, press ganging Rumpkin into service, she found she could make a cosy enough nest providing she didn't need to move anywhere or do anything. Which tended to suit her just fine anyway since it gave her an excuse not to tear herself away from her book.

The sofa and armchair both had their backs turned to the front door, creating a sort of half wall that sectioned off the living area from where their coats and shoes lay haphazardly by the stairs. The walls of the living area were lined with bookshelves. Until recently, the shelves had actually been quite bare; Julia had preferred to borrow her books rather than buy them. But when Biddle's library closed down, she'd liberated a large number of books that were either her favourites to reread or on her extensive to-read list. She preferred to think of this less as stealing from her erstwhile employer, and more like taking in rescue animals, à la Rumpkin.

Even so, only around half of the shelf space contained books, the rest containing framed photos of family and holiday snaps and various little trinkets and mementos that had been collected over time. A colourful hand-painted mug from Majorca was Sally's latest addition. It nestled next to the empty plant pot which used to have a cactus growing in it. Between them, Julia and Sally had neglected to water it for so long it had finally given up the ghost and wilted away, joining the long line of house plants that had failed to survive the women's stewardship. The grass and nettles in the back garden were the only plants that managed to thrive at the property, often reaching hip height before one of them gave in and borrowed a lawnmower from the family over the road.

The few patches of wall that weren't covered by bookcases, or photographs of the two women and their friends, were painted a vivid crimson colour. The beige that their landlord had chosen had been painted over in a clandestine operation when they realized he'd given up on the semi-annual house inspections. He had conducted one when they'd moved in together about three years before and never bothered since.

A smell began to waft through from the kitchen, tantalizing Julia's nostrils. Sally had disappeared in there twenty minutes before saying she was making tea and hadn't returned. Eventually curiosity and hunger got the better of Julia and she emerged from underneath the woollen blanket and poked her head round the kitchen door.

Sally was in there, bent over the oven just removing a tray of something Julia couldn't see. But the recipe for brownies lay open on the kitchen counter and Sally wore an apron pronouncing 'Do Not Approach Without Chocolate', so Julia felt she could make a shrewd guess as to what was in the tray.

"I don't think that's a very nutritious tea, Sally," said Julia sternly.

Sally pointed a spatula at her. "I'm still on holiday rules," she said. With that she scooped the recipe book out of the way with her elbow, apparently heedless that it landed on the floor in front of the oven, and placed the steaming tray down in its place. She then thrust the spatula into the middle of the bake.

"You know they'll just come out as a gloop if you don't leave them to cool," Julia said.

"Don't care. Hungry now," Sally replied and dolloped a large heap of substance that couldn't quite technically be called a brownie onto a plate. "Do you want any or not?"

"Please don't ask stupid questions," Julia replied. "It's a waste of your time and mine."

Sally ladled another scoop onto a second plate and passed it to Julia.

"Are you on holiday, too, then?" Sally asked as she watched her friend pick up a teaspoon and make good inroads into her serving. Julia's old schoolfriend had slightly more of the local accent than her, although like Julia it tended to phase in and out depending on who she was talking to and how much she had drunk.

Julia licked some liquid brownie from her bottom lip. "When you only average six hours of work a week, every day feels a bit like a holiday," she said.

When the library had shut its doors for the last time she found out the hard way that Biddle Rhyne wasn't exactly a hub for employment. The convenience store off the high street was the only place where she had found any work and each time she did a shift in the fluorescently lit shop she felt a little bit of herself withering away like their old cactus.

Sally hadn't bothered with a teaspoon and was delving into her plate with her bare fingers, which meant there was a substantial delay before she was able to reply. "No luck getting Mr Donaldson to up your hours then?"

"Not yet, the old skinflint," Julia replied.

Sally inserted the last of the brownie from her plate and sucked her finger clean. "Wow. I missed this," she said.

"Missed what exactly?" Julia asked, chasing the final bits of brownie around with her spoon.

"You know," Sally said, indicating the mostly empty tin of brownies. "Simple honest home cooking. Holiday's nice and all, but it's nice to be back, too. I'm looking forward to everything just being normal again."

Chapter 4

Julia paused before the turning to Forge Lane, not quite able to bring herself to approach the flapping strands of police tape and relive the memories of the crashed car and the grizzly victim that she'd seen the day before. Still, she was sure this was close enough to make no odds.

It had been chilly when she left the house so she had worn her long grey coat with the fur around the collar, and it kept out the wind that had built up its head of steam over the moors and battered against the side of the hill. She pulled her phone from her handbag – the dull brown one chosen because it was the only one which went with her thick coat.

She tapped a few buttons on her phone to bring up the stopwatch and hit 'go'. Then she spun smartly on her heel and headed back down the hill at a brisk walk, her arms swinging stiffly at her sides. With each step she saw a little puff of her breath, but despite this she was still quickly heating up inside her coat. It was a good coat. Well, it should be, given what she'd paid for it. Or rather, what her mum had paid.

At first the hedges rose up high on either side, bare and bristly at this time of year, and shot through with twisting vines of ivy. Her view ahead was restricted to a narrow slice of the fields that lay to the south of the hill, and the sparse, waterlogged moorland beyond that.

But as she turned a dogleg in the road, the hedges fell away to waist height and the panorama opened out. She could see her target, the Barley Mow, below: the whitewashed, thatch-roofed old coaching inn sitting by itself on the country lane just outside the village.

And next to it was Biddle Rhyne itself. The nearside was lost to sight to Julia, nestled against the side of Pagan's Hill, but she could see the medieval heart of the village. There was a string of buildings, large and small, that had survived through the centuries and now formed the high street. Spanning out from that were the lines of residential streets built in much more recent times and home for most of those who lived in the village, including her. On a rise of slightly higher ground just beyond the houses was the large brick structure of the village hall, the green with the duck pond set in front, and on the edge just before the moors rose the tower of St Mary's church.

The view was soon lost from sight as she marched down the hill and turned another bend, so Julia concentrated on her walk, keen to set as good a time as she could.

She was mildly out of breath and perspiring under her clothes by the time she lifted the latch on the Barley Mow's door and stepped inside. She regretted wearing her thick coat now and quickly unbuttoned it and hung it up on the iron peg by the door, before huffing her way over to the bar, her short stature giving her no cause to duck underneath the beams.

Julia flopped her handbag onto the top of the bar and then leaned heavily against it as she caught her breath, flapping the neckline of her jumper trying to encourage some air movement.

Sally watched with an amused expression from the other side of the bar. She was dressed in the regulation black top which she always claimed was unflattering on her body shape, although Julia secretly disagreed with this. Sally bent forwards to whisper conspiratorially. "How long?"

Julia unzipped her handbag and rummaged through, retrieving her phone. She thumbed the button to pause the stopwatch. "Twenty-eight minutes," she wheezed.

"Hm," Sally replied thoughtfully and drummed her fingers on the bar. "Do you think Barry could have shaved a few minutes off your time?"

Julia peered surreptitiously over Sally's shoulder to where the man in question stood slouched against the doorway to the kitchen. He was a tall man, and quite flabby, with a completely clean-shaven head. Somehow the pub's uniform always looked particularly rumpled and dishevelled on him. He was currently glancing down at something hidden in his cupped hands, presumably sneaking some time on those awful mobile phone games that he seemed to be addicted to.

"I doubt it," Julia said. "That was as fast as I could go without breaking into a run. I saw him come back in through the door and he wasn't out of breath. At least, no more than he usually is, the chimney. As far as walking goes, no, I don't reckon he could outpace me."

"Because he's a fat tub of lard?" Sally said, and not particularly quietly.

Julia saw Barry look up at this comment. When he saw Julia looking back at him, he scowled and stalked off into the kitchen.

"Well, if Barry's in the clear then who does that leave?" Sally asked.

Julia bit her bottom lip. "There are plenty of people with a motive, but I can't think who would have had the opportunity. And then, there's that strange man."

"Strange man?"

"You know what I mean. The man I didn't recognize. Who spent the whole day sitting in here drinking for no reason."

Sally put a daft voice on, mimicking their old schoolteacher. "Yeah, spending the day in a pub enjoying a couple of pints. What a weird thing to do."

"Well, who else could it have been?" Julia hissed.

"Wait and see what the police come up with?" Sally suggested.

Julia let out a laugh. "DI Jones? From what he said, he's just going to sit with his feet up and wait for someone to turn themselves in for it. No chance."

"What will you do now, then?"

"I don't know. Something will turn up. But right now I'm going to go over to the garden centre and retrieve that note. If the ineffective detective does ever get off his backside and treat this as a you-know-what investigation then I don't want that sordid thing turning up with my fingerprints plastered all over it."

"Sneaking into a deceased woman's office, is that a good idea?" Sally asked.

This gave Julia pause. It was rare that Sally was the voice of caution so it was probably worth paying some heed to it. "No, I'm not sure that it is. But right now I think the only obvious person with the opportunity to steal the old duffer's car keys is me, and if Biddle Rhyne's Finest do figure that out as well, then I don't really want an incriminating note becoming Exhibit A."

"Fair enough," Sally replied.

Julia's heart rate had returned to normal now but she was still flustered and plastered in sweat. "How about a tap water before I tackle that hill?" she asked.

"Sure." Sally turned to get a glass from the stack when a voice stopped her.

"No tap water unless it's a paying customer," Ivan said, his timing impeccable, as he wandered through from the kitchen towards the dining room.

Julia scowled at the man's back as he departed.

Sally threw her hands up helplessly. "Boss's orders," she said.

"I know, I know," Julia muttered and went to retrieve her coat.

* * *

Julia crested the top of Pagan's Hill and stood leaning against a stone wall with one palm, the other resting on her hip. Once more she was out of breath and sweating heavily. She had meant to make the ascent a gentle stroll and recuperate a little after the power walk earlier on, but when she'd passed by the turn-off for Forge Lane and the tattered police tape snapping in the breeze, she'd been spooked and put distance between her and the crash site as quickly as she could.

From the top of the hill the countryside was spread before her bathed in the late afternoon light: an expanse of fields criss-crossed with drainage rhynes that stretched all the way to the wooded hills in the distance. There were little trails of movement where herds of cows traversed leisurely across the pastures, and high overhead a bird of prey circled, watching vigilantly for mice below. It was only a suggestion of a bird's shape at this distance, but when the wind blew the right way its cry carried all the way to Julia, clear as the day itself.

The bucolic vista was interrupted only by the glass walls and corrugated-metal roofs of Only Gardens which lay at the foot of Pagan's Hill and spread out towards the countryside, its nurseries lining the edge of the nearest fields.

She was just soaking in the view, allowing it to calm her rattled nerves, when a head appeared over the stone wall making her shriek in fright and rendering the preceding exercise rather pointless.

"My apologies, dear girl, I didn't mean to startle you. I was just doing a spot of gardening." The major's gruff voice was ameliorated somewhat by his kind words.

Julia regathered her wits and waved his apology away. "Don't mention it, Major. It's not your fault; I was miles away."

The major gave a broad smile. "Perhaps you'd like to step into my garden for a moment? I could make us a spot of tea. That's always good for calming down, I find."

Julia returned his smile. "I'm far too warm for tea. But a glass of water would go down a treat."

The major indicated at the little wooden gate just down the lane and Julia reached over to flick the catch and stepped through.

She'd not been in the major's back garden before. Situated on the flank of the hill, it fell away sharply, but just by the gate the ground had been levelled off into a patioed terrace on which there was a little wooden table and a brace of matching chairs.

The major waved his hands at the chairs. "Take a seat and I'll fetch the drinks."

Julia thanked him and the major made his way back uphill towards his home, pressing his hands heavily onto the top of his legs as he went, each step accentuated with a grunt. Julia settled back into the seat and took in the view again. It was much the same as she had seen from the lane, but the garden centre was now hidden behind the high hedge at the end of the major's land. All that was visible of Only Gardens was the riot of colour from their nursery, perfectly punctuating the plainer landscape beyond. Julia sighed contentedly. Lack of employers aside, living in Biddle Rhyne did have its perks.

The major reappeared after a short interval, carrying in wobbly hands a circular metal tray with a jug of water on it and two tumbler glasses. Julia noted with pleasure that there were half a dozen or so ice cubes floating in the water and the sides of the jug were beaded with condensation. She greedily gulped down one glass and poured herself another.

It dawned on her that they'd been sitting in silence for some time and suddenly realized that she was making quite the poor guest. "It's a lovely garden you have," Julia said, glancing around.

"Thank you," the major replied. "I do consider myself to be somewhat green-fingered."

She'd only said it as something polite to fill the silence, but it was true nonetheless. The lawn was mowed to perfection and little apple trees lined the near end by the road, bursting with fruit. A small border ran along the far side of the garden. It was fairly empty now but presumably a bit more lively in the summer months.

Julia placed her glass down on the wooden table and then it struck her that she had an opportunity here to pursue her sleuthing. "Say, Major, do you know who the bloke was in the pub yesterday? Red-haired man sat over by the bay window. He was there for a few hours, I think."

The major turned his head from the view over the countryside and looked at Julia. "Oh, you're the girl who was behind the bar, aren't you?"

Julia's heart sank. If he didn't recognize her after all that they'd been through the previous day then the chances of him recognizing some man from the pub were slim to none.

The major wiped some water from his moustache with the back of his hand. "Yes, I recognized him. Can't say I've ever spoken to the chap, though. I see him in the Fox and Hounds quite a bit. He's usually there for the meat raffle on Thursdays."

Julia couldn't help but laugh. The old duffer didn't remember the woman who'd driven him home and discovered a fatal car crash with him, but of course he'd remember someone from the local whom he'd never spoken to.

"Why do you ask?" said the major.

She didn't want to rile him up by mentioning his stolen car. "Oh, erm, someone dropped a quid yesterday. I was just wondering if it might have been him. Wasn't you, was it?"

The major shook his head. "Not me. You should just pop it in that collection tin for old donkeys or whatever it is."

"I'll do that," Julia said. She made a mental note to put a pound of her own into the tin when she was next at the Barley Mow. It felt somehow like robbing a charity otherwise. Apparently she was fine with lying to spare the major's feelings but dragging a charity into it was where she drew the line.

Julia finished her water and thanked the major again. She pulled the gate shut behind her, and feeling much refreshed she wended her way down towards the garden centre. She would go and retrieve that note with her fingerprints on it and then she knew it would feel like a long wait until Thursday to question the mysterious red-haired man.

Chapter 5

Julia waited for the short string of traffic to make its way past before quickly hurrying across to the opposite pavement. The B-road that skirted the edge of Pagan's Hill was about the closest that the village of Biddle Rhyne came to being busy. The garden centre was just off the road, its sprawling car park stuffed full of cars, as it always seemed to be.

Beyond, the tall red letters proclaimed 'Only Gardens' and the cluster of glass-sided buildings gleamed in the sunshine.

Julia made her way through the automatic sliding doors and through the rows of pot plants and a sales display of various large, shining gardening implements. Although the gaudy orange sign above them said they were 'garden essentials', by and large Julia wasn't certain what they were for exactly, and certainly couldn't name them. Shoppers, mostly older than her, streamed by on either side pushing rattling trolleys before them, loaded up with all manner of different products. Despite its name, Only Gardens sold a surprisingly large array of clothes, kitchen goods, pet accessories and home ornaments, all at a substantial mark-up.

Off to her left, towering high above the shoppers, was a needlessly large pyramid displaying Lance Teller's earthenware. Julia was about to hurry on by when she spotted Janice, Lance's wife, standing in front of it. She had always been somewhat fascinating to Julia, having been a few years above her at school and was then, as now, achingly pretty to look at: a small, poised figure with blonde hair cascading down almost to her waist and the delicate bone structure of a model. She was also something of a free spirit; somehow it seemed very natural, maybe inevitable, that she had ended up living in the old farrier's cottage on the side of the hill.

Janice was standing almost with her back to Julia, apparently fascinated by her husband's pots. Julia's heart went out to her, it couldn't have been easy turning a blind eye to Lance's affair for all these years, even if it was putting food on their cottage's table. She couldn't recall ever seeing the pots on sale anywhere else.

Julia sighed and carried on through the garden centre leaving Janice to her thoughts.

When she reached the far wall, Julia pretended to read in detail the instruction label on a set of carpet-cleaning gadgets, and when she judged the coast was clear she slipped through the swinging door marked 'Employees Only' and emerged back outside at the rather utilitarian rear of the garden centre.

She'd made this trip once before, a week ago. She'd been walking Rumpkin in the woods on Pagan's Hill when without warning, and quite out of character for the normally docile creature, he'd bolted away, barking his little head off and ignoring Julia's cries of 'heel'.

In the ensuing forty-five minutes she'd searched high and low around the woods, calling his name, until another dog walker said he'd seen a little terrier roaming free and generally getting in people's way in the garden centre car park.

Relief filling her heart, Julia had hurried there and arrived quite out of breath but found no sight of her beloved pet. Instead, she spotted Mrs White as she was climbing into her car and the woman informed Julia that the dog had been 'barking in a threatening manner' and had scared away potential customers, probably costing her several thousand pounds in business. Furthermore, Mrs White had said that Rumpkin was locked in her office and would remain there until she had been reimbursed in full for her lost revenue, and with that she had slammed the car door, gunned the engine and sped away in a shower of gravel.

Julia had watched, fuming, as the car disappeared, before taking matters into her own hands. She slipped through to the back, prised open the sash window to Mrs White's office and clambered in.

There she was reunited with Rumpkin, but found him chained on a short lead to a filing cabinet in the corner. She'd needed to unwind a paper clip and pick the lock in order to move the handle and finally free Rumpkin.

As the grateful pooch covered her face in canine saliva, Julia went to shut the drawer again when a piece of paper on the top had caught her eye.

It was a death threat – the anonymous kind made by snipping letters out of magazines and pasting them onto a side of A4. It simply read 'CARRY ON AND I WILL KILL YOU'. Julia had picked it up and puzzled over it for a few seconds before shrugging and returning it to the drawer. Perhaps the boss of a place like this, especially if that boss was a cow like Mrs White, got dozens of those notes a year. Probably more than she got Christmas cards. At the time, Julia hadn't thought for a second that the threat might be made good on.

And now Julia found herself standing in the office once again, this time needing to retrieve the threatening note which was covered in her fingerprints. At the very least she could wipe them off, she realized, and then maybe call anonymously to the police and tell them about the note.

She fished around in her handbag and found her sunglasses case still in there from several months ago when the weather was a little less British, and took out the little square cleaning cloth.

She scanned over the little office desk in the corner until she found some paper clips. They were plain grey, of course, Mrs White would never deign to use colourful ones, Julia reflected as she began to unspool one.

The lock on the drawers fought back a bit harder than she remembered it doing the previous time, and it took her a few moments of jiggling her improvised lockpick about before she was rewarded with the satisfying click.

She slid the drawer open and swore under her breath. No sign of the threatening note. She quickly grabbed the sheaf of papers that were there and leafed through them, but it was definitely gone. All this effort for nothing, but still at least she wouldn't have to worry about DI Jones finding it here, having a case of detectile malfunction and fingering Julia for the crime.

She was just giving the sheaf of papers in her hands one more flick through to make sure when she realized just what she was looking at and stopped.

"Bloody hell," she whispered to herself.

The papers were a proposal, apparently a quite advanced one, for a rebrand and expansion of the garden centre. The council had given their blessing to expand the car park and put up another, larger building behind the existing ones. And worst of all, the egomaniacal Mrs White had decided to rebrand the enterprise as 'White's Only Gardens'. And somehow the razor-sharp minds of Biddle and District Parish Council hadn't seen the obvious problem with that. Perhaps, Julia thought, she needed to add 'racially motivated' to the list of reasons to bump off Mrs White.

She was just considering the extent of the poorly thought-out rebranding exercise when she heard the sound of keys jingling in the door lock and her heart skipped a beat. She quickly stuffed the plans back into the drawer, bolted across the room and, with a complete lack of poise or dignity, propelled herself out of the window, her legs kicking and bicycling behind her as she wriggled out and onto the gravel outside.

She was just reaching up to pull the sash window closed behind her when the office door opened and Mr Smedley stepped through into Mrs White's office. He stood in the doorway with an oversized coffee mug steaming away in one hand and blinked several times at Julia.

Julia fluttered her hand up to give him a little wave and did her darndest to smile casually.

Mr Smedley was the deputy manager at Only Gardens. A rake-thin man with a short crop of greying hair on his head who insisted on wearing a name tag with 'I'm here to help' on it, despite it not being part of the uniform. He'd risen up from the garden centre's ranks to officer class, gaining his promotion in the field after one particularly fraught Christmas Eve shopping spree when the card reader had packed in.

With a look of befuddlement on his bespectacled face, he crossed the office and pushed the window up again. "Julia? What in heaven's name are you doing back here?"

Julia intensified her smile as the gears whirred away in her brain. She held up the dinky little glasses cloth that was still clutched in one hand. "Mrs White used to chuck me a fiver to clean the windows once a week," she said.

Mr Smedley looked intently at the cloth and then shrugged. He put the coffee mug down on the windowsill and pulled an overstuffed black wallet from his trousers. He pulled a five-pound note out and holding it in two fingers he offered it towards Julia.

Slowly, not breaking eye contact with Smedley, Julia reached out and took hold of the note, depositing it loose into her handbag where it would probably never be seen again.

"I guess we can keep the arrangement going now that it's my office," Mr Smedley said in his thin, reedy voice.

"Your office?" Julia said. Jumping into Mrs White's blooming grave was what she thought.

"Yes, well. I am in charge here now." Smedley puffed up his chest. Julia noticed that his nametag already read 'Manager' rather than 'Deputy Manager'. A brand-new tag too, not just the old one with a word crossed out. He certainly hadn't wasted any time.

Julia thought about pointing out the crassness of his, presumably self-appointed, promotion but decided better of causing a potential scene. She nodded a quick goodbye and scuttled off, emerging back onto the shop floor from the employees-only door with her head down and weaving through the crowd as quickly as she could towards the exit.

When she stepped back out into the fading sunlight, a car horn blasted from a nearby parking spot and she saw Sally, her face hanging out of the car window, framed by her lustrous curls, and her arm waving to attract Julia's attention.

Julia beetled her way over the gravel and slipped quickly into the passenger side.

"Was it a success?" Sally asked as she revved up and pulled away, swinging out onto the main road and causing the approaching van to halve its speed as the car struggled to gain momentum, burdened as it was by two entire women. "Did you get the note?"

"It wasn't there," Julia said.

"You think she handed it over to the police?" Sally asked, turning the headlights on as they drove into the shadow of the hill and dusk thickened quickly around them.

"Maybe. More likely she just put it in the bin, though, I reckon. If she did give it to the police, then it doesn't seem like the detective I spoke to ever got wind of it. And do you know what else? That cheeky swine Smedley has already promoted himself to manager and moved right into Mrs White's office."

Sally gave a shrug. "Well, why not? He saw the opportunity for advancement, I guess."

"Can he advance, though? I mean Mrs White owned the place. She must have some family knocking about somewhere. It's not like she's going to give it to Smedley because he was deputy manager."

"She's got a daughter," Sally replied. "She was in my brother's year at school. I'm still friends with her on Facebook. She emigrated to Australia years ago. I'm constantly seeing photos of her living her best life on some beach or other. I doubt she'd be coming back to get hands-on running the family business and freezing her backside off every winter. She probably will want Smedley to run it."

Julia gasped as a thought struck her. "What if Smedley hastened things along?"

"What? Bumped Mrs White off so that he could be top dog?"

"Well, yeah, why not?" Julia said.

"But you didn't see him in the pub on Sunday, did you?"

"True. He'd still have had to find a way to pinch the major's car keys, wouldn't he? But maybe he got someone else to do it for him. Like that red-headed stranger. He could probably afford to pay them a decent whack, whoever he got."

Sally gave this some thought as she continued to ignore the traffic around her. "It's possible, I suppose. I'll give you that much. But if the redhead stole those keys for anyone, I'd say Janice Teller is way more likely. She's the one who might really want to hurt Mrs White. Or Lance. He's always had a temper, hasn't he? I could see them having a lover's tiff."

"Speaking of the redhead," Julia said, "I've got a lead on him. How would you like a trip to the Fox and Hounds on Thursday?"

Chapter 6

They detoured on the drive home to pass through the centre of the village. The road was straight here but little wider than the country lanes, meaning that the traffic only proceeded at the pace of the slowest road user, usually a tractor or, in this case, a cyclist. Julia usually welcomed the sedate road when she was driving; a pleasant relief from the blind corners of the lanes and the speeding motorists encountered there. But the slower pace never came naturally to Sally and she impatiently huffed and drummed her fingers on the steering wheel as they crawled along, eventually hauling the car into one of the bays at the side of the road so that Julia could hop out.

Julia made her way down the pavement at a brisk walk. Not that she was in any hurry, but Sally would be keen to get home. Fair enough after working her shift.

The high street was an odd mixture of buildings. On Julia's right was a medieval tithe barn, its buttressed stone walls stretching thirty feet down the street. Long ago it had been converted into dwellings, and little wooden front doors, each painted a different, cheerful colour, broke up the stone at regular intervals. Once she was past the barn, there was a short terrace of Victorian houses, three storeys tall and each with a jutting bay window. A tabby cat sat lazily in one of them watching Julia pass. She resisted the temptation to wave.

After that the pavement widened out. In the space left by previous generations of builders was a more recent, glass-fronted building, set back a bit from the road. Originally it had been built as the village post office, but a few years ago the villagers had been told, to their surprise, that they didn't post letters after all and the post office was swiftly converted into a hair salon. But in the space in front still sat the bright red pillar box and, more importantly, the matching red phone box.

The outside of the phone box was pristine and the warm yellow light shone out from the latticed windows, pooling onto the pavement tiles. But when Julia pulled the door open she was dismayed to find the entire interior was coated in a thick layer of grimy dust and spiderwebs hung in great nets from the ceiling. She shuddered; evidently even in a backwards-looking place like Biddle Rhyne mobile phones had still caught on with the locals.

Searching her purse, she found that she still had a single pound coin wedged in the bottom, offered up a silent prayer of thanks, and then dropped the coin into the slot and dialled, heedless to what bacterial diseases her fingertips were being exposed to in the process.

The phone rang a few times and then a woman's voice answered, sounding bored. "King's Barrow Police Station. How may I assist your call?"

Julia put on a deep throaty voice as a disguise and thickened her otherwise mild local accent. "Detective Inspector Rhys Jones, please. I have some information about the Audrey White murd– the Audrey White hit-and-run.

The voice on the phone remained monotone. "Please hold."

Julia waited, tapping her foot on the ground, for what seemed like an interminably long time until a familiar Welsh voice spoke on the phone. "This is DI Jones."

Julia spoke, deepening the disguise on her voice even further. "Detective. I think you should know that there was a death threat against Mrs White. An anonymous note threatening to kill her. The note's gone now but I think you should treat this as a possible murder investigation."

There was a pause on the other end of the line followed by some heavy breathing. "Julia Ford, is that you?"

Julia pushed the handset away to arm's length and looked at it aghast like it might try and bite her. "No!" she squeaked and quickly slammed the receiver back onto its cradle.

With a patter of feet she ran back down the high street towards the waiting car, her hair flying out behind her as she went.

* * *

The doorbell went off, just as Julia had been expecting it to for the last two hours. The gentle melody chimed throughout the house, although today Julia found it anything but calming.

She had been reading the end of *Rebecca*. A woman caught up against her will in a legal investigation had seemed nicely appropriate. Maybe she, too, could brazen her way through this. Not that it helped much in the end, she thought.

The doorbell rang out again, stirring her from her thoughts. She shut the book neatly, placed it on the armchair and took a deep breath before extracting herself from the blanket and making her way to the front door, shooing away Rumpkin who stood with his tail wagging on the doormat.

"Inspector," Julia said, doing her best to smile.

Jones's broad face remained stony. "May I come in, Miss Ford?"

Julia considered saying 'no', but the last thing that she needed was him turning up again with a warrant, so she reluctantly stepped aside and ushered him in.

Jones stood silently just inside the door, steadfastly ignoring the small terrier that was jumping up to lick at his fingertips. He looked around the living room as though he might spot any number of death threats pinned up on the walls.

Julia scooped Rumpkin up and clutched him close to her chest. He turned his attentions to his mistress and began licking the underside of her chin. She kept his wriggling body gripped firmly in her arms.

"Shall I make tea, Inspector?" she asked, straining to keep her lips out of Rumpkin's reach.

"Thank you, that would be nice," Jones replied, without turning to look at her.

She hovered for a moment more and then beetled off into the kitchen, kicking the door shut behind her with her heel and bending to deposit Rumpkin softly onto the kitchen floor where he got distracted by a row of crumbs alongside the oven. Evidently Sally had cooked something before heading back to the Barley Mow for the evening shift.

Julia filled the kettle and as she watched it rattle away to itself on its stand, she was painfully aware that she'd left a copper unsupervised in her living room. Not that she had anything incriminating to find, but the idea made her uneasy, and she willed the kettle to hurry.

As soon as the water was boiled, she rushed through into the living room carrying a tray holding the stripy red-and-yellow teapot, two cups, a little jug of milk and a bowl containing the last sugar cube in the house.

When she entered, Jones was sitting with his legs spread apart in her favourite chair looking rather miserable but otherwise at home. Well, he probably looks miserable most of the time he's at home, Julia thought. Rumpkin snuck in on her heels but he had lost interest in the visitor now and trotted over to lie down in his basket in the corner.

The teapot lid rattled as Julia set the tray down onto the side table, her nervous hands trembling slightly. Jones sat looking at the contents of the tray as one might look at a particularly challenging cryptic crossword clue or a sudoku where you know you've put a number in the wrong place but can't work out exactly where.

"And what brings you to my little home, Inspector?" Julia asked, keen to break the silence and get this over with.

The policeman's head swivelled up from the tea tray to look at his host, his jowls following shortly afterwards. His pale-brown eyes regarded her with a slow, reptilian-like blink. "A certain phone call I received at the station."

"Oh, yes?" Julia said, hearing her voice rising in pitch, powerless to stop it.

"Yes. A phone call regarding a threat against Mrs White's life. You wouldn't know anything about that, would you, Miss Ford?"

Julia shook her head rapidly, tousling her dark hair in the process.

"I seem to recall that at the scene of the incident you did mention that you knew of people who might have been less than fond of the late Mrs White."

Julia raised a finger into the air. "I said that she wasn't popular. Not that I knew of any people in particular."

Jones let out a wheeze and rubbed at his oversized nose with the back of one of his index fingers. "Ah. Nobody springs to mind, then?"

Julia paused for a moment before answering. She felt like she was going against her better judgement in talking to Jones, but the lengthening silence was oppressive. "Everyone knows Mrs White was having a fling with Lance Teller," Julia said. She knew neither of the Tellers had been in the pub that day, but that didn't mean someone couldn't have filched the keys for them, like the red-haired stranger.

Jones looked decidedly unimpressed. "Miss Ford," he said. "Those two had a business arrangement."

"That's not what I heard. It's common knowledge why she was running off to his cottage every week," Julia said.

Jones gave a belaboured sigh. "It was also his workshop. Mrs White's iPad has dated minutes of their discussion on the day of her death. It makes tedious reading unless you're really interested in pottery sales. Anything further would seem to be unsubstantiated gossip."

Julia shook her head again. She didn't believe for an instant that discussing sales was all they got up to that morning. They were hardly likely to minute it, though.

Jones stared at her for what felt like a considerable time while Rumpkin snored happily away in the corner.

"You know," Jones said, finally, his gaze still fixed on Julia, "I was wondering to myself, as you do, who would have had the chance to steal the major's car. In the business, we call this 'opportunity'."

"Ah." Julia sighed. So the inspector wasn't as close-minded as she had feared. Maybe he would listen to her after all.

But before she could continue, Jones cut her off by clearing his throat loudly and said, "You do realize that means you, don't you, Miss Ford?"

"Me?" Julia said. "But I was behind the bar the whole time."

"Now that's not really true, is it?" Jones said.

He looked at her expectantly as her mind raced, but she had no clue what he meant. She really had been manning the bar the whole day.

Jones's face remained neutral but Julia couldn't help but feel he was enjoying himself. "I gather you went to change one of the barrels. It took you an unexpectedly long time, I hear."

For a second Julia found herself lost for words. "You've been speaking to Barry," she said wretchedly when the power of speech made its way back to her.

"I have," said Jones. "And what an interesting conversation it turned out to be."

"I was gone two minutes, if that," Julia said. "Ask the major, he'll tell you."

"Oh, I did," said Jones, "but he doesn't remember."

"He doesn't remember how long I was gone," Julia muttered to herself, cursing her luck.

"No," said Jones. "He doesn't remember you, period. He's convinced it was the other girl serving."

Julia's mouth gaped. "But I was working," she said.

"I know that," said Jones. "That's why I know you had the opportunity to steal the major's keys."

Julia swallowed. All of a sudden she felt faint. "Are you going to arrest me?" she asked weakly, knowing even as she said it that it made her sound guilty.

"No," Jones said. "I need some concrete evidence first. A death threat matching your handwriting would make my life easier. But failing that I expect I can dredge something up."

"The death threat was clipped from magazines," Julia muttered under her breath.

"What was that?"

"Um. If you think I wrote that note, why would I have phoned you?"

"Well, the note's gone," Jones said. "It wasn't there when we searched Mrs White's office. Some killers like to lead the police on a wild-goose chase, you see? They think it's a game. I don't find it fun, though."

Julia swallowed and found herself without a reply.

Jones shook his head and rose to his feet. "It's been nice talking to you, Miss Ford. Don't get up, I'll see myself out. Thanks for the tea."

Julia instinctively glanced at where the teapot sat steaming, completely untouched.

Despite the inspector's words she trailed after him and watched Jones make his way down the drive, alongside the knee-high grass that passed for a front lawn. After she shut the door behind the inspector she put her back against it, willing herself to be calm. She wondered whether he knew about her argument with Mrs White in the garden centre car park. They hadn't exactly kept their voices down and there was no shortage of people about to overhear. She had better find who had stolen the major's car and fast. Otherwise she anticipated another visit from the charming detective.

Well, as far as sleuthing went she would just have to wait until the Fox and Hounds' meat draw. In the meantime, Julia felt that she needed to calm her nerves a bit. She looked again at the stripy teapot and the two matching cups.

No, this called for something stronger. She grabbed a coat and a scarf from the pile under the stairs and began pulling her trainers on.

"Come on, Rumpkin," she called, waking the slumbering animal. "We're going to the pub."

* * *

Her familiar route took her along the edge of the housing estates that hugged the edge of the village. Maybe not the most picturesque of homes, especially at this time of year when their gardens were all bare and lifeless, but they looked homey enough; a few of them already had deep yellow lights shining out through drawn curtains.

Thoughts kept rushing around and around in Julia's head, mostly concerning the detective inspector, his poor manners and his even poorer detecting skills. It seemed like she was going to have to find who had written that horrible note if she was going to prove to Jones that she hadn't made it herself. But where to start? She could only hope that the red-haired man would be able to provide her some answers.

Reaching the end of the street, she squeezed her way through a little alleyway between two houses, tall wooden slat fences hemming her in on either side. Unkempt brambles spilled over from one side and dangled down, making her lean sideways as she walked, and even then her dark hair snagged on the thorns. As much as she would have liked to get angry at whoever let their garden become such a menace, her own lawn was doing its best impression of the Lost Gardens of Heligan, so she knew she couldn't really throw stones.

The alleyway came out onto the country lane leading towards the Barley Mow. On the far side of the lane was a weed-covered drainage rhyne, and beyond that fields stretched away into the distance. A few brown cows were slowly making their way across them in search of choicer grazing.

The rain started when she was halfway down the lane and she pulled her brolly from her handbag and snapped it up before carrying on. For once it wasn't too windy for it to stay up, despite the open fields stretching away to her left. Normally she just resigned herself to getting wet. After all, it made a good excuse to sit next to the open fire and nurse a glass of wine. But her encounter with Jones had put Julia out of sorts and she wasn't sure that even the Barley Mow's house red was going to fully fix things.

Rumpkin didn't seem to share his mistress's concerns and he trundled along at her heel, merrily splashing in and out of puddles apparently without even noticing. Julia watched despondently as his fur turned wet and matted in the rain. He would be making good use of the fire at any rate.

They had just rounded the final bend in the road when a little white Peugeot came barrelling into sight, its engine growling over the rainfall. Julia did her best to hustle Rumpkin off the road and pin the dog between her shins as the car carried on past, oblivious to them.

The car rushed by, the muffled thump of its stereo audible, and one set of tyres clipped a deep pothole, sending a spray of muddy droplets into the air and all over Julia's jeans and the bottom of her coat.

She swore to herself. If she'd been but a few years more senior, she might have considered turning around and shaking her fist after the receding car. No matter what other things he was completely wrong about, Jones was right about the joyriders in this part of the world being a complete menace.

"Come on, boy," she said wearily, releasing the entrapped Rumpkin. At least the pub's nearby, Julia thought, as she slogged down the last hundred yards or so of the lane, hopped over the long brown puddle that had formed at the edge of the road and crunched over the wide expanse of gravel to the front door.

Unsurprisingly for a weekday evening, it was quiet inside. No customers at all, in fact, in the parlour, although Julia could hear some voices drifting through from the dining room next door.

Sally looked up from whatever she had been doing on her phone and slid it into the back pocket of her work trousers, giving Julia a smile. "Hello, chicken," she said, "you look wet."

"I feel wet," Julia said. "We both need to dry off."

Rumpkin went padding along the floor, his claws clicking on the flagstones and his nose to the ground investigating the smells that had accumulated since his last visit. But predictably he trundled over to the fire and lay down on his side with his belly basking in the dull glow coming from the logs.

Julia watched him go and then clambered up onto one of the trio of leather-padded stools at the bar and plonked her handbag down. The jingle of loose change brought her mind back to her earlier conversation with the major and she drew a pound coin out of her purse.

She picked up the charity collection tin and turned it round in her hand to examine it before putting the coin in. She was greeted by a photo of a frolicking little donkey, faded with age.

"Feeling rich, are we?" Sally asked.

Julia shrugged and dropped the coin in. By the sounds of it the tin was otherwise empty. "What can I say? I have a soft spot for animals."

"Even that one?" Sally asked. She sent a scowl in Rumpkin's direction. Already the smell of wet dog was beginning to fill the parlour, but Julia knew Sally was just being playful.

"It's not entirely his fault," Julia said, "some vagabond in a Peugeot covered us both in puddle water."

"Drivers these days," Sally gasped. "If only they were all as cautious as we are."

"I know. And look at what that idiot did to my jeans," she said, holding her leg out straight and pointing at the smattering of mud.

Sally duly leaned over the bar to inspect them. "A capital offence, I'd say. No trial, just straight to hanging."

"I couldn't agree more," Julia said.

"Now knowing you, you won't be drinking at this time in the afternoon," Sally said, as she pulled a bottle of the house red out from under the bar and began pouring a glass.

Julia took it graciously and took the first, wonderful sip that reminded her that all bad things would pass.

Just as she was swallowing, the kitchen door swung open and Ivan strode through on his way to the dining room. Despite the diligently ironed shirt and the carefully knotted tie, he always looked rumpled and out of kilter, probably because he charged circles around his pub all day.

Without breaking stride, he pointed at the drink in Julia's hand. "I hope you're charging her for that, Sally."

"Of course, Ivan," she sang back merrily as he disappeared through the door.

She gave Julia a shrug which meant 'better pay for this one, then, he'll be checking.'

Julia sighed and pulled her purse back out. "Pity he can't come up with some more shifts, the cheapskate," she said, holding her card to the contactless reader.

The dining room door opened again, a little chatter of voices audible for a moment, but this time it was Barry coming through. He slapped a scrap of paper down in front of Sally and then lent his elbow on the bar. "Drinks order for table five," he said.

"You could do it yourself, you know," Sally said as she pulled the receipt from the card reader and put it into the till.

Barry just shrugged. "Nah."

Sally shook her head and began gathering glasses for the drinks.

Julia regarded Barry as he stood waiting, staring vacantly into space. She wanted to be angry with him for what he'd said to the inspector. But knowing Barry, he was too dim to realize what trouble he'd put her in. It would be like being angry with a puppy, really.

She sighed. "How are you liking the waiting job then, Barry?" she asked.

"I'm not," Barry said, keeping his voice down. He must have already learned Ivan's uncanny knack for appearing whenever someone complained. He raised his finger up. For a moment Julia thought he was going to pick his nose, but he saw her watching him and lowered it again, twiddling his fingers together to keep them from mischief. "Beats being unemployed, though, I suppose."

"That's true," Julia said. "If you think of packing it in here let me know, I want to be first in line for the applications."

"Fine. But I won't be shifting unless something better comes along," Barry replied. "You heard of anything?"

"If I'd heard of anything I'd be applying myself," Julia pointed out.

Barry pulled a face.

Sally finished pouring the drinks and placed them onto the circular plastic tray. "Maybe when the garden centre expands you can get a job there again, Barry," she suggested.

"Nah, that won't happen," Barry said. "Smedley's all against the idea of expanding. Reckoned it would bankrupt the place. I heard him and Mrs White arguing about it before I got the can."

"Somehow I can't imagine Smedley arguing with anyone," Julia said. He was such a drippy person that she didn't think he had any fight in him.

Then again, she did fancy him for Mrs White's murder, and if that were the case, then even if he didn't get his hands dirty himself he must still have a more ruthless side that he kept hidden.

Barry continued. "Oh, yeah. He got proper passionate about it, he did. If there's one thing he loves, it's that bloody garden centre. He didn't think there were enough punters for the expansion. No way he's going to sign off on it now that Mrs White's... well, you know."

The door slammed open forcefully and Ivan materialized again. He took in the scene of Barry leaning idly against the bar next to the full tray of drinks. He took a deep breath to keep himself from yelling. A vein throbbed gently on his temple. "Barry. Drinks order. Now," he said through gritted teeth, and then backed into the dining area.

Barry righted himself and picked the tray up, sloshing the contents of several lagers onto it. "Better get back to it then," he said, ambling back into the dining area. "Smells of wet dog in here anyway."

Sally watched him go. "Don't worry, Julia, it wouldn't surprise me if he got canned from here, too. Although, do you reckon we could stand working together as well as being roomies? You might get sick of me. Or would I get sick of you first?"

Julia wasn't listening. "Interesting what he said, though. If Smedley thought the expansion would be the end of his beloved Only Gardens, then that's one more reason he had for seeing Mrs White bumped off."

Sally nodded her agreement, blonde curls bobbing. "And one more reason for us to go to the meat draw. I'm quite looking forward to that, it's been ages since I've had a decent steak."

"We're meant to be looking for a potential murderer for hire," Julia said firmly, "not getting you a slap-up dinner."

"We could do both," Sally replied. "Anyway, have the fuzz been to visit you yet?"

Julia took a long drink of wine before she replied. "Yes."

"I take it from your tone that you didn't convince the detective of your innocence, then?"

"I don't think I did myself any favours with that anonymous phone call," Julia mused.

"Don't worry, chicken. I believe you're innocent."

"Thanks. Hopefully you won't have to be my character witness."

"No. Not with all the horrible things I know about you."

Julia scowled, contrasting her friend's angel-sweet smile.

She was trying to think of a witty retort when her handbag beeped at her and she stuck her hand in to find her phone. She saw a missed call from Mr Donaldson.

"Oh, blast it," she said, thumping her drink back down on the bar.

Only one shift of work in the whole week and she had managed to forget all about it. She blamed Jones and his meddling for throwing her off. Muttering curses about him and all his profession she clicked her fingers at Rumpkin and headed for the door. Outside, the sound of falling rain had grown heavier.

Chapter 7

The Fox and Hounds was located on Biddle Rhyne's high street. Not that the sleepy village had much in the way of nightlife – or daylife for that matter – but this was the closest approximation that it had. While the Barley Mow on the edge of the village made most of its income from food, the Fox and Hounds was more of a straight-up, no-nonsense drinking pub. Although there was a decent array of brass-topped pumps and taps, its menu was limited to various flavours of crisps and, if you were lucky, maybe a pickled egg or some pork scratchings.

When Julia and Sally stepped inside, the pub was already decently busy. The little square tables of dark wood were about half occupied and a few groups of people propped up the bar as well.

Julia had dressed up for the occasion, more because she hadn't been out in the evening for a long time than because the pub really warranted it. She was wearing a strappy top, her best-fitting jeans, and had taken the effort to curl her hair with moderate success. She had always been mildly envious of her friend's ability to throw on any top she liked, even one that hadn't managed to make it through the wash, and instantly look ready for a night out anywhere as long as she paired it with a decent pair of heels and a handbag.

Julia put that thought from her mind and scanned the room for her red-haired target but couldn't spot him anywhere. "The night's still young, I guess," she muttered.

"It is indeed," Sally replied at the top of her voice. "Now come on, let's get ourselves a drink."

With that, she took Julia by the elbow and guided her through the tables and past the whitewashed walls adorned with pictures of red-coated men on horseback in various stages of the hunt. They took their place between two knots of punters, both of them apparently pretty well soaked already.

The beleaguered-looking chap behind the bar desperately manned the pumps as he tried to keep up with the orders being flung at him from all directions. A line of gin bottles, every colour of the rainbow, sparkled on a raised shelf under a pair of spotlights. Sadly, they were about the only dash of colour in the dingy room.

As Julia stood, shuffling impatiently and waiting to catch the barman's eye, she noticed the major standing further on down the bar wearing one of his familiar corduroy suits. He spotted the two women and raised his half-full pint glass to them.

"Hullo, Sally," he said cheerfully before turning back to watch the TV which was mounted in one corner of the room.

Julia shook her head. Unbelievable.

After they'd been served their wines, Julia led the way to the back of the room where there was a raised wooden platform. At various times it had housed a pool table and a stage for open mic nights, but now it stood rather forlornly with a couple of tables shoved in while it awaited the landlord's next money-making idea. But from the elevated position, Julia could better observe the comings and goings of the pub, so she and Sally perched there on high stools keeping vigilant eyes on the room.

By the time their glasses were empty, the room had filled up even more and one by one even the other tables in their little snug became taken. But despite the influx of people there was still no sign of their quarry.

Julia checked the time on her phone and then shoved it back into her handbag. "Do you think the meat draw's on today?" she asked Sally. "The website said 7.30 but it's almost 8.00 now."

A man on the neighbouring table turned round to them. He was wearing a plain white T-shirt but he wore it well for all its plainness, and Julia couldn't help noticing the muscles underneath it. He was clean-shaven and the matching closely shaved head made it difficult to pin down his age, but she'd have put him a few years older than herself and Sally.

"Don't worry, it's always late to kick off," he said. "You two have entered, have you?"

"Nope," Sally replied.

The man looked puzzled. "Well, why do you care if it's on or not?"

He has a point, Julia thought.

"I'll go and enter now," Sally said and she slid down from her bar stool and disappeared elbows first into the growing throng at the bar.

Julia watched her go. "She's, um, very forgetful, my friend," she said to the man by way of explanation.

He chuckled and held out his hand. "I'm Mark," he said.

Julia returned his handshake and introduced herself.

"You sound like you're a regular, then. For the meat raffle, I mean," said Julia.

Mark shrugged. "Sometimes. Makes me cook some different things if I end up with some odd bits of meat. But it's a bit of a way to come for me."

"You don't live round here, then?" Julia asked.

"Not really," Mark said. "I'm in King's Barrow."

"That'll be a fair old trek back for you then," she said.

She realized to her mortification that he might take that as an invitation to come back with her, but she needn't have worried, any seedy inferences sailed over his head.

"My dad will pick me up, I live with him," Mark replied and then looked a bit sheepish and took a pull from his drink.

"Nothing wrong with that." Julia smiled.

Mark opened his mouth to reply but was interrupted when Sally came thundering back up onto the raised area, waving a long chain of red paper tickets manically in front of Julia's face.

"Bloody hell, woman, how much meat do you want?" Julia gasped.

Sally let the tickets flutter to the table and waved the question away. "They wouldn't make change. But never mind that, look!"

Julia followed her friend's finger through the crowd to the doorway.

And there he stood. He was middlish height and wore a baggy-fitting striped polo shirt. His features were difficult to make out in the half-light of the bar but the shock of gingery-red hair on his head was unmistakable.

"That's him!" Julia squeaked in excitement.

"I know it's him, let's go get him," Sally hissed back.

Julia allowed Sally to grab her hand and pull her from her seat, and the two of them pushed through the crowd towards the stranger.

The man was standing at the back of the loosely formed queue for the bar, apparently content to wait his turn. Julia hesitated as she reached him, wobbling for balance on her heels as she teetered to a halt, and then summoning her courage she reached up and tapped him smartly on the shoulder.

Several inches taller than her, the man turned and looked down at Julia, a wary expression on his face. He gave an indistinct grunt of acknowledgement. Julia couldn't tell if he recognized her from Sunday or not.

"Hi." Julia gave him a warm smile.

Now that he was there in front of her, she realized that tracking a potential murderer down to the local pub might not make the top ten list of the best ideas she'd ever had, but here she was so she figured that she might as well press on. And besides, she told herself, Sally was right there if anything turned south. She cleared her throat and did her best to stand tall. "Do you remember me?"

"Afraid not," the man replied, but Julia was certain she'd seen a flicker of recognition in his eyes. He started to turn back towards the bar.

Julia carried on before he could turn his back on her, practically shouting to make sure he couldn't ignore her. "Go on, you must remember me. From the Barley Mow? I served you drinks all afternoon."

She was sure now that he knew her, it was nothing less than fear that went over the man's face.

"You're wrong, I was never there that afternoon!" the man yelled, the colour in his face rising to match his hair. "Now, if you'll excuse me, I need to go."

With that, the man pushed through, bumping both Julia and Sally roughly on the shoulders as he barrelled through in the direction of the exit.

Julia laid a hand on his shoulder, only lightly, in the hope of changing his mind. "Wait," she pleaded.

The man spun back; he had a harrowed, desperate look on his face now. "Leave me alone," he snapped.

His hand shot out and he gave Julia a shove. It wasn't particularly hard as shoves went, but in her heels it was enough to topple her over and she landed heavily on the stone floor of the pub with a gasp.

No sooner had she landed than several hands were reaching down to help her upright. She saw both Sally and Mark peering down with concerned expressions.

She shrugged away from their grasps. "Don't mind me, I'm fine. Get after him!" She gestured wildly at them like someone trying to scare away a goose.

Sally and Mark exchanged a look and then hurried towards the door, Sally struggling somewhat in her heels, the contents of her low-cut top bouncing, but Mark made better progress and his long strides soon had him out the door.

Julia clambered back to her feet, reassuring various well-wishers and onlookers that she was indeed fine. By the time she'd managed this, Sally and Mark were reappearing through the doorway and she could tell by their faces that they hadn't caught him.

"He got away, the git," Sally fumed, planting her hands on her hips as she caught her breath. "Jumped right on the Number 7 bus as it was pulling away."

"What rotten luck," Julia said.

"I know. One bus in the whole evening and it turns up just in time to spirit him away."

"Any chance of you telling me what this is all about?" Mark asked, looking at the two women in turn. "Old boyfriend?"

Julia snorted. "Hardly. You've heard what happened to Mrs White, I suppose?"

Mark nodded. "Poor woman. I used to work in the garden centre, back in the day. What a terrible accident."

"Well, that's just it." Julia sighed and then she beckoned him towards their table at the back of the pub.

Once there, she filled Mark in on what had happened, about how someone had stolen the major's keys, finding the threatening note, and her suspicions that what happened to Mrs White might not have been an accident after all. Despite the wine loosening her tongue, she opted to leave out a few choice details about her own breaking and entering as well as exactly why Mrs White was up and down Pagan's Hill every Sunday.

Mark listened intently to Julia's words and at the end of it he settled back into his chair, tapping his fingers thoughtfully. "I don't suppose you've thought of taking any of this to the police, have you?" he asked finally.

Julia rolled her eyes. "Yes, but the man who passes locally for a copper, the boneheaded DI Jones, doesn't want to hear any of it. At first he was content to put his overburdened feet up and wait for some joyrider to have a change of heart and turn themselves in. Now he's taking the note seriously, but because I'm the one who reported it, he thinks I wrote it."

"Did you?"

"No!" Julia snapped.

"All right, all right, I believe you. Even if the boneheaded DI Jones doesn't."

"You know the man, do you?" Sally asked.

Mark gave a wry grin. "I am familiar with him, yes. And I'll admit he's not the sharpest knife in the drawer."

Julia studied the lad's grin, wondering if perhaps he had a dark past that he hadn't revealed yet. But before she had a chance to ask, the door banged open, the handle chipping away at the existing hole in the plasterwork. A giant of a man staggered in, holding enough cling-film-wrapped parcels of meat to feed a small army.

"Sorry I'm late, here I am," the man called out.

There was a half-hearted cheer from the pub crowd as he made his way over to the bar and deposited his load on top of it.

"Right." He rubbed his hands together, his booming voice carrying easily over the background chatter. "Let's get this meat raffle underway, shall we?"

The rest of the night rolled on pleasantly enough. The drinks flowed and as the numbers were called Sally's long string of raffle tickets converted themselves into a fair-sized heap of meat, stacked into an unstable-looking pyramid on the table.

"I'm not sure we're going to be able to get all of this home," Sally said, looking the pile up and down.

She's right, Julia thought, there was more than a couple of large armfuls there to carry and she didn't fancy stuffing her handbag full of raw meat.

Julia plucked a pack of sausages from the top of the pile and offered them towards Mark. "I can't interest you, can I?"

He broke into a broad smile. "It's not often I come to the pub and a girl offers to slip me some meat at the end of the night. It's normally—"

He didn't get a chance to finish, he was cut off by a plopping sound as Julia slapped him on the chest with the sausages. "You cheeky beggar."

Sally hid behind her painted nails as she laughed. "You guys! I've heard of 'meet-cutes', but this?"

Mark chuckled. "No, I don't want any meat, thank you. But my dad will be here any moment now, I'm sure he can drop you and your winnings home."

Between the three of them they managed to scoop all of the prizes up and stumble their way out of the pub. Waiting on the pavement just outside was a silver sedan car with its engine idling and its sidelights on. The door opened and the driver stepped out.

"Hi, Dad!" Mark called.

Julia looked on in horror. Standing on the pavement before them, one elbow propped on the roof of his car, was the voluminous form of the boneheaded DI Jones. He looked typically thrilled to see Julia.

"Dad?!" Julia shrieked.

With that she turned on her high heels and ran screaming in the other direction, parcels of meat tumbling from her arms as she went.

Chapter 8

Julia awoke to the smell of sausages frying downstairs. On the one hand: warm, cosy duvet. On the other hand: that scent was stirring something in the deep, primitive parts of her brain. With a sigh, she rolled from her bed and did her best to transition from duvet to dressing gown without exposing herself to the nippy morning air.

She followed the smell to the kitchen, still blinking the sleep from her eyes. She took a spot next to the stove, soaking in the warmth and the aromas as Sally prodded the fat, herb-infused bangers around in the sizzling pan. Still, Julia drew the line at letting her mouth hang open with her tongue lolling out; she could leave that to Rumpkin.

"That smells so good," Julia murmured.

Sally chuckled and continued to poke the sausages about the pan. Over the top of her fluffy pink dressing gown she was wearing a 'Kiss the Chef' apron, already well covered in grease splatters. "What makes you think you're getting any?"

"Tease." Julia stuck her tongue out at her friend before catching sight of Rumpkin from the corner of her eye and quickly retracting it. Another scent caught her nostrils and she padded over to the cafetière. "Ooh, fresh coffee. You are spoiling me this morning."

"I thought you could use the pick-me-up," Sally said as she artfully flicked the sausages from the pan with a knife and onto the waiting slices of bread.

"Why?" Julia asked, watching suspiciously over the top of her sandwich as she took a bite and instantly covered the inside of her mouth in burning-hot sausage fat.

"The memorial service is in an hour," replied Sally.

Julia swore, but the word was muffled through a mouthful of half-chewed sandwich. She'd forgotten about the memorial service. The vicar had arranged one in honour of Mrs White, since apparently it was going to be a while before her family could reassemble from around the globe to have the proper funeral. He felt it would help the community after 'losing one of its pillars'. Julia hadn't quite been sure if he'd meant it. That was probably the cynic in her, this was the vicar after all.

The sun shone as Julia and Sally made their way through the village. Their route took them past the Fox and Hounds – the heavy, deadbolted door shut tight at this time of the morning – and down the length of the old high street. Something squelched underfoot and Julia realized she had stepped into a cellophane-wrapped burger patty.

"My smartest shoes," she said to herself and sighed.

Finally they diverged from the main road and down the causeway that led to the immaculately mown village green. Ducks milled about happily on the grey surface of the water, and on the other side the church tower rose majestic and solid into the overcast sky. At the very top, above the delicate crenellations, the flag of St George snapped and curled in the stiff morning breeze.

On each of the four sides of the tower was a grotesque: strangely contorted faces wrenching their mouths wide open with their hands. In wet weather the rainwater would come gushing out of their misshapen mouths and spatter onto the ground. Unfortunately, some medieval craftsman, either through lack of forethought or through malice, had positioned one of these grotesques directly above the main door. Presumably after centuries of pious congregations getting soaked by the outlet every time it rained on a Sunday, the water had been redirected by means of an incongruous white section of drainpipe which came out of the statue's mouth in an L-shape and deposited the water just to the side of the doorway instead. And thus it was that the moss-covered piece of pipe was the only defect in the otherwise flawless example of a rural parish church.

The bell was just chiming the hour as they crossed the green, so they hurried on towards the great oak door, joining the trickle of other late arrivals. Julia and Sally passed under the maw of the grotesque and into the church before quickly settling in on the rearmost pew.

The church was a bit under half-full, by Julia's reckoning. Not a bad showing, she supposed. Most of the faces she didn't recognize, but she would guess they were related to the garden centre in one way or another: employees and suppliers. There was also a handful of attendees around Mrs White's age, probably her friends, assuming Mrs White had such things, and several full rows near the front of older folk. Julia thought that they might be the church's regular congregation.

It had been a long time since she'd been in here, Julia reflected. Her mum used to take her at Christmas before she'd moved away from the village. She shifted on the bench and fidgeted distractedly with the order of service. She wasn't really the pious type, and in all honesty, she hadn't felt any desire to attend the memorial, but since she had been there when the body was discovered, she felt in a strange sort of way that she was obligated to attend. At least Sally, ever stalwart, had offered to go along with her for moral support. She glanced over to smile at her friend before turning her attention to the front of the church.

The vicar, a slightly pudgy man of middle years, his black hair flecked with grey, stood at the lectern. To one side of him was a surprisingly large number of wreaths and other floral tributes, heaped into a tall and colourful pile with a few of the more expensive-looking arrangements given prominent places at the front. Julia couldn't help thinking that all the garden centre employees would have got them at a fairly steep discount and then chastised herself for being so uncharitable.

To the other side of the vicar was a large easel holding a black-and-white portrait of Audrey White. Even in this photo she looked stern and disapproving, her close-cropped grey hair framing an austere and lined face. It would seem that despite the circumstances no one had been able to unearth a picture with her smiling.

As the final peal of the bells echoed away, the organ struck up, filling the vaulted stone church with music. It sounded somewhat off-key to Julia, but since she was neither a churchgoer nor musically inclined, she was left wondering if that was how it was meant to sound.

The organ music, as it could loosely be termed, was in full flow when someone bustled in from the rear door and squashed into the vacant seat next to Julia.

She turned, ready to direct the offending person into one of the roomier pews in front when she saw who it was. "What are you doing here?" she hissed over the warblings of the pipes.

Mark glanced over at her. She was sure that she could detect a faint smirk on his lips. "I'm here to pay my respects to a beloved pillar of the community, the same as you, I'm sure."

Julia huffed and looked straight ahead, resolved to ignore the man, when she realized that she was glaring daggers at the vicar and forced herself to relax. It might have been her imagination but the vicar seemed to have caught her eye and was looking back questioningly. Julia gave a quick smile and then remembered she was at a memorial service and tried to look mournful instead.

Mark leaned over so their shoulders were touching and whispered. "Why did you run away from me last night?" he asked.

"You know why," she hissed back, trying to keep her voice down. She took a deep breath.

"Because of my dad?" asked Mark.

"Of course your bloody dad!" Julia snapped.

The large hat in front of her turned around to reveal the head of an elderly woman. She raised her finger to her lips. "Shh!"

Julia pursed her lips shut.

"I did protest your innocence to him on the drive back. But he said that the innocent ones never run."

"I am innocent!"

"Shh!"

"You should tell my dad that."

"I told you, I did!"

"Well, try harder."

Sally swivelled around in her seat, raising her finger. "Shh!"

"Shh! yourself, you tart!"

"Shh!"

"Can we go out again?" Mark whispered.

"We didn't go out before!"

"Shh!"

"Then can we go out for a first time?"

"No we cannot!"

"Shh!"

"Shut up, Sally, I mean it."

The vicar's baritone voice rose up, cutting over the chatter at the rear of his church. "As I was saying, Mrs White was a warm, generous lady. Beloved by all those who knew her, or worked with her…"

"Now be quiet, you're getting me in trouble," Julia said in the meekest of whispers.

"If you agree to go out with me then I'll be quiet," Mark said, his voice somehow even lower than Julia's.

"That's harassment that is."

"Yes, probably."

"Fine. Fine! Just shut up."

The woman in front held her finger up again. "Shh!"

"You shut up, too."

The elderly woman gave an angry glare but turned back to the vicar who by this point was staring openly at the group. "And our thoughts and prayers in this awful time are with her family who are, as we speak, making their arrangements to return back home to mourn," the vicar said, his voice almost at a bellow now.

Julia zipped her mouth and resolved to listen to the vicar. He extolled Mrs White's virtues at some length, to the point where Julia began to wonder if he'd ever actually met the woman he was eulogizing. After the third or fourth time she'd been told how warm and wonderful Mrs White was, her mind began to wander and she started with horror to think about how her first date with DI Jones's son might go down.

He was his father's son, and surely the apple couldn't fall far from the tree. But, she reasoned, if she played her cards right then she would possibly be able to win the detective over to her side. She had to admit that she'd never been great when it came to endearing herself to boyfriends' parents, even when she'd had easier starting points than literally being suspected of murder.

And the problems didn't end with suspected murder. There was nowhere to date in Biddle Rhyne. The garden centre café was probably the most happening spot that the village could lay claim to.

Add on the facts that Julia had nothing to wear on a date, no witty repartee of conversation and no appreciable amount of money to spend, and it all began to look rather hopeless.

Julia's chain of thought was disrupted as the vicar snapped his weighty Bible shut and climbed down from the lectern. There was an awkward pause punctuated by one or two coughs from the congregation and then there was a hushed conversation from the front pews. Mr Smedley stood up, looking about him as though he was uncertain where he was, and then ascended the little wooden spiral of steps to take the vicar's place.

Mr Smedley stood looking at the assemblage, blinking, the overhead lights gleaming periodically off his spectacles as he swivelled his head left and right. His black tie was knotted tight underneath his throat but somehow lacked the meticulously neat look he normally exuded when Julia had seen him at the garden centre.

At long last, he produced a crumpled sheet of paper from his back pocket and did his best to unfold it as it stuck to his hands. He cleared his throat and then began to speak. His reedy voice didn't quite carry as far as the back of the church and the words were lost to Julia, although she guessed that she could probably fill in the content for herself. What a great mentor Mrs White had been, what a great loss to the Only Gardens family it was.

About midway through his speech, Mr Smedley pulled a spotty red handkerchief out of his jacket and began to mop his brow. Julia realized she'd never actually seen anyone do that before in real life.

He was nervous, there was no doubt about that. But was it just public speaking that was giving him the willies? Certainly, Julia had seen him address half a dozen or so inattentive minimum-wage garden centre employees at the start of a shift, but she supposed that speaking to a church full of mourners was something else.

Perhaps, Julia thought, peering intently at the man's beetroot-coloured face, he's nervous because he knows more about Mrs White's final hours than he's let on, and he's struggling to keep the façade up?

There was a stir of movement all around her and Julia saw the gathered congregation all getting up from their seats. Apparently the service was over. From the tower above, the church bells chimed the half-hour, although how Mr Smedley and the good reverend had filled thirty minutes with nice things about Mrs White, Julia had no idea.

She rose and followed the flow of people as they filed out of the side door of the church and into the fresh morning air. It seemed they'd timed the service to just miss a rain shower because the flagstone path leading away from the church gleamed and the smell of recent rain floated up from the churchyard.

The vicar stood by the exit, shaking hands with people as they went by and exchanging pleasantries.

Mark turned to her as they waited in the queue, shuffling forward in short, awkward intervals.

"So how about that date, then?" Mark prompted.

"What about it?" Julia replied, pointing her chin in the air and trying to keep her demeanour aloof to the whole thing, all the while hoping that Mark might have some better ideas than she did.

"You mentioned you have a dog, didn't you? I do, too, we could take them for a walk."

A dog owner. Well, that scored him a point in Julia's books. That put him on one point. No, that was unfair, he'd scored a point or two for the way he'd looked in the muscle-fit shirt last night. Sadly she'd had to deduct some points from his score based on the presumed genetic deficiencies he must surely have from his father's side.

"Fine," she said.

"Say midday tomorrow?"

"Fine."

He flashed his grin again. "I could call on you? I can always get your address from Dad."

Julia scowled. "Or not. We can meet with the dogs at the top of Pagan's Hill." That was nice, neutral ground.

"Perfect." Mark reached the front of the shuffling queue, gave the vicar's hand a perfunctory shake, and made his way down the path towards the gate.

The vicar had been beaming at his departing flock as they filed by, but when Julia reached the front of the line, the vicar's expression turned icy. She couldn't begin to imagine why.

All the same, she gave her best smile and struck up conversation with him, in the hope that Mark would lose interest and buzz off by the time she'd finished. She wasn't sure that she could deal with any more of his jibes before she was fully caffeinated for the day.

"What a wonderful service, Reverend," Julia gushed.

"Ah. I'm glad you thought so," the vicar replied, ice melting just a smidge. "Was there any particular part that struck a chord with you?"

Julia's mind scrabbled briefly for something, anything, to latch onto. "Well, I did like the organ music at the start," she replied. "It was very moving, I thought."

The vicar's face dropped again. "Hm. Interesting. We were missing our usual organist, unfortunately. Mrs Teller declined to play today, saying she had a prior engagement. I would have thought that given the occasion she might have been able to move things around, but oh well."

Of course, Julia had forgotten that Janice Teller was the premier organist here. No wonder she didn't feel like playing the organ to memorialize the woman who was slipping away every Sunday to play with her husband's.

"Yes, Janice plays here every Sunday morning," Julia mused out loud.

The vicar sniffed. "Well, almost every Sunday morning. She missed the last one as it happens."

Julia's heart leapt. "Wait a second," she said, rather more loudly than she had intended. "When you texted me you said that she was in church last Sunday."

The vicar's eyebrows rose heavenward. "That was you who sent that text, was it? Well, she did attend, but she came to the afternoon service instead. Although we get such a paltry turn-out in the afternoon these days that there's really no point prepping the organ for it. A waste of her talents, definitely." He couldn't keep the bitterness out of his voice. "Still, she had a good excuse, I guess. She was helping at some OAP's birthday lunch, I think. Something like that. Anyway, how come you were so interested in Mrs Teller's attendance?"

"As I said, I'm a connoisseur of organ music," Julia replied. "Must be going; bye, Vicar."

She locked arms with Sally and marched her quickly away down the path before the vicar could piece together that none of what she had said to him made any sense whatsoever.

Sally, suddenly finding herself being propelled along, stuffed her phone back into her handbag as her feet scampered to catch up with her torso. "What on earth's the matter?" she said.

Before Julia could reply she had reached Mark who was waiting for them, leaning against the rough stone wall that bounded the churchyard. He smiled as the two women approached. "That was a nice chat you were having. I didn't realize you were a churchgoer."

By the time he'd finished speaking Julia was already through the gate and past him, Sally being towed along behind like a badly hitched caravan fishtailing behind a car. "Must dash, toodle-oo," Julia sang, waving to Mark with her free hand as she careened on towards the pond. The ducks exploded out of the water with fright and went quacking into the sky.

"What is all this about?" Sally demanded, finally pulling back and putting up some resistance. "Stop it, I can't run in these heels."

Julia relented and slowed the pace to a more genteel walk. "Didn't you hear what the vicar said about Janice Teller?"

Sally shook her head. "You were being boring, I was playing *Candy Crush*."

Julia sighed, but she was too excited to be annoyed at her friend's poor sleuthing abilities. "The vicar said that

Janice was only at the afternoon service, not the morning one like she usually is."

Sally's eyes began to widen into large circles as this sunk in. "But that means–"

Julia couldn't wait for her to finish. "That means she doesn't have an alibi after all."

"But you still didn't see her at the pub, did you? So how would she have gotten hold of the major's car keys?"

"That's just it," Julia said, her words tumbling out rapidly. "She was at the pub. The vicar said she was helping with the OAPs' lunch, it must have been at the Barley Mow. She's such a tiny little thing, if she came in with the whole busload of pensioners then she could easily have been hidden in the crowd and swiped the major's keys as she came in. She would have known he'd be there, she'd have seen him there after church often enough."

"Okay," Sally said, "so she swipes the keys. But then what? You didn't see her leave?"

"Once she had the keys, she could easily have gone out the back way by the loos. Then it's about twenty-five minutes to drive up, do the deed, and scamper back down the hill as fast as she can and return to the restaurant by the back door again."

"Twenty-five minutes in the loo?" Sally asked.

Julia shrugged. "It would be embarrassing. But no one's going to ask too many follow-up questions, are they?"

"I suppose not," Sally conceded.

"Come on." Julia gave her friend's arm another tug. "We've got to question her."

"We could let your boyfriend's dad do that," said Sally.

"No, stuff that," Julia replied. "I think it should be someone competent."

Chapter 9

With Sally in tow, Julia set off enthusiastically across the high street, waiting impatiently at the crossing for the green man while she rehashed her theories about Janice Teller.

After crossing the road, they turned up one of the residential streets, wending their way along the cut-through to the foot of Pagan's Hill.

But by the time they had squeezed through the tiny gap in the hedge onto the muddy footpath, Julia discovered that enthusiasm was no substitute for a decent pair of walking shoes. Her heels, diminutive as they were, made for slow going up the slope, and every ten steps or so she'd lose her footing and be forced to fling her arms out for balance, looking rather like a small child playing at being an aeroplane. At one point, even this was not enough and she slipped down onto one knee, coating her tights in bits of wet grass, and she swore so loudly that she sent the previously docile flock of sheep skittering off across the field, their red-marked tails bobbing up and down as they went.

Julia turned from watching the sheep and looked back down the hill. Sally was lagging behind but despite her slower ascent Julia couldn't help but notice she was mud-free. She looked down at her own ruined tights. There was something possibly worse than mud on there and Julia did her best to dislodge it by shaking her leg about.

Sally came puffing up alongside. "Come on, Julia, not time for resting now, we're almost there."

Julia scowled darkly at Sally's back and then scampered over the tussocky slope to catch up with her.

Eventually, the footpath reached a five-bar gate that led onto a paved road and Julia wrenched at the spring-loaded handle. There was a groan of metal but nothing budged. She tried again, grabbing the metal in both hands and leaning her body weight backwards. It seemed the gate had been designed for the use of someone much stronger, perhaps a weightlifter or a professional rugby player.

Julia threw her arms up in despair.

"This was a bad idea," Sally stated, leaning over the gate to look up the lane towards the Tellers's cottage.

"Yes. Thank you, I am aware of that," Julia replied.

"We could always turn back. Come up here again this afternoon. Maybe drive."

Julia sighed. "We're practically there."

"Fine," Sally said. "But if things go south then don't say I didn't warn you."

Together, the two women managed to haul the handle back on the gate and it swung open with a reverberating screech.

The Tellers's cottage sat on its own patch of land, maybe half an acre or so in size. The cottage itself was an old stone building of one storey, its red-tiled roof uneven and wavy in a way that was lovely and quaint, but in no way would Julia have trusted it if she had to live under it.

As she made her way up the winding tarmac track, she had to admit that Lance had done a wonderful job with the place. She remembered playing up here when she was a girl. Back then, no one had lived in the cottage for decades. The whole place had been crumbling and surrounded by choking weeds and giant stinging nettles. When Lance had bought the cottage he'd fixed the whole thing up with his own two hands, only calling in occasional favours from people he knew.

Now the place shone. The mortar between the stones was refreshed and trellises of roses adorned either side of the door. The old poured-concrete yard had been pulled up and replaced with paving which was now home to a little wrought-iron table and two chairs, arranged to look down the hill over the view of the sheep fields to the village at the bottom. A chimenea sat next to the table, with a waist-high pile of chopped wood beside it, nestled under a sturdy-looking shelter erected against the wall of the house.

Smoke was rising from the cottage's chimney and the sound of birds singing floated down from the trees at the back of the house. The whole thing would seem the very definition of idyllic rural living if Julia wasn't aware of the fractured marriage that the cottage housed.

"Go on, you knock. I'm not doing it," Sally said petulantly, and Julia realized that she'd been standing in front of the cottage, lost in a trance.

Evidently Lance didn't want anything as crude as a doorbell to spoil the rustic façade of the cottage, so Julia raised her hand and rapped hesitantly with her knuckles on the untreated wood door. Immediately after she could hear the sound of someone banging around inside and then the door swung inwards.

Instead of Janice Teller as she'd been expecting, it was her husband, Lance, who stood in the entranceway. Julia realized that she hadn't planned for this, or indeed at all, and she stood there staring at him, slack-jawed.

Lance frowned out at them, cutting a sinister figure in the dim light of the cottage. It couldn't be often that they had unexpected guests up here on the side of the hill, especially not two women in formal dresses and mud-splattered high heels, and he didn't look pleased to see them.

"Yes?" he asked, his voice gruff but not aggressive. "What do you want?" He planted a hand on the doorframe. Obviously he wasn't about to be inviting them in for tea.

He was older than Julia, maybe in his mid-thirties. He was tall and broad-shouldered, wearing a black shirt with the top couple of buttons undone revealing a V-shaped section of chest. He was square-jawed, apparently hadn't found time to shave this morning, and his dark hair was long but not unkempt with just a few flecks of grey in it. The phrase 'chiselled good looks' sprang unbidden to Julia's mind. In other words, when pictured against the scowling and lined face of the late Mrs White, it didn't take a master detective to realize that they could only be knocking boots in order to shift Lance's product.

Julia opened and shut her gob a couple of times before managing to stammer out, "We're after Mrs Teller. I mean, Janice. Is she home?"

"No," Lance replied, "she's not. Anything I can help you with?"

His manner was brusque and implied he'd rather not be helping them at all. His eyes, which Julia noted were rather bloodshot, darted between the two women who stood on his doorstep.

He could help, of course, if he was able to provide an alibi for his wife. Or even if he could just confirm whether she'd been at the Barley Mow on Sunday or not. But even Julia's limited sense of tact told her that question wouldn't go down so well. Her mouth again opened and shut without any words appearing.

Lance's face knotted together into a scowl and he jabbed a finger in front of Julia's face. "Don't think I don't know what this is about," he spat.

"Pardon?" Julia managed to squeak out.

"Don't play dumb with me. Poking your nose into other people's business. Treating our lives like it's some sort of seedy gossip column for your amusement. Well, you're not going to get anything from me. Leave me alone. Leave my wife alone. If you come sticking your long noses up here again, you'll regret it, mark my words."

Julia swallowed. The wind blew in and suddenly it felt like they were very alone, up here on the hillside. She couldn't help but remind herself that Mrs White had been killed not a few hundred yards from where they were standing.

"S– sorry, Mr Teller," Julia stammered, a vertigo feeling flooding in as her instincts screamed at her to turn and run while she forced herself to stand there and politely take the tirade.

Lance Teller gave a final glare, his eyes smouldering. "Beat it," he hissed, before slamming the door so forcefully that the sash windows on either side rattled in their frames.

Sally and Julia exchanged the briefest of glances with each other before turning and retreating back down the path. At first, they set off at a fast walk, but by the time they had reached the gate to the Tellers's property they were in a full run, hurling themselves down the hillside in a blur of movement, clutching their hands together for both stability and reassurance that they were both still there and in this thing together.

Only when they got back to the lane and round the corner, with the cottage and its irate inhabitant out of sight behind the tall hedgerow, did they allow themselves to stop and catch their breath. Their hands still clutched together, they stood panting and gasping for the chill autumn air.

"That did not go how I had wanted it to," Julia said.

Despite it all, Sally couldn't help but roll her eyes. "He was not pleased to see us. We didn't even ask him any questions and he went off like a flipping bomb."

Julia looked back in the direction they'd come, although of course all she saw was the tangle of the hedge. Still it felt like she could almost sense him still. "He's angry about something."

"What if his wife was the one who hit Mrs White? Do you think he knows?" Sally asked.

Julia shook her head to say she didn't know and began the long trudge back down Pagan's Hill. "Maybe. Or maybe he did something to Mrs White himself."

"Why would he, though?"

"I don't know," Julia said, gradually beginning to feel like herself again. "A lovers' quarrel? Or she threatened to end it with him. He certainly seems to have a temper so maybe something like that could have tipped him over the edge. But if he did run her down then he'd have needed his wife's help to get the major's keys."

"Do you think Janice would have helped him?"

"No idea," Julia said. "I think we need to speak with her, though."

Although it wasn't that cold, Sally pulled her coat close around her. "Well, I don't know where to find her. And I'm certainly not hanging around here waiting for her to come home to her darling husband."

"Agreed," Julia said.

"We could ask at the Barley Mow when it opens? See if Barry or Ivan saw her. I think he's working today," Sally suggested.

Julia scrunched her face up. "Even if they saw her there it doesn't tell us much. We need to know if she disappeared for any length of time. Like twenty-five minutes or more."

"And you don't reckon our lads would have been that on the ball?"

"Sadly, no. Ivan would have been shooting in and out, he would have been gone way longer than twenty-five minutes himself. And Barry wouldn't notice if Janice brought a cow in with her. But there is somewhere else we can go to find out what she's been up to."

"Oh?"

"The retirement home. The one that booked the trip to the pub. We can call there and see what they can tell us about Janice's whereabouts on Sunday."

"Fine. Let's go back and get changed first, though, please. And a shower wouldn't go amiss either."

"No argument here. And I'll need to borrow one of your earrings, too."

* * *

Abbot's Mead retirement home sat towards one end of Biddle Rhyne's high street, at the far end from Pagan's Hill, where the land became flat and featureless. It was a fairly sizable brown-stone building, painted white at the edges. Originally it had been a pair of handsome Victorian houses but back in the seventies they had been knocked through and converted into a care home.

Its twin bay windows looked out on the small but well-kept lawn with a tangled crab-apple tree set in the centre of it. As autumn drew on, the tree bore dozens upon dozens of little round fruit and they had attracted a family of crows, which scattered, cawing, into the air as Julia and Sally made their way up the tarmac path towards the main entrance.

When the heavy, power-assisted doors closed behind them shutting out the traffic of the high street, the care home radiated a subdued, peaceful hum. The pine-topped front desk was unstaffed and Julia could see through the Perspex screen into the office behind where a woman in a starched white uniform sat with her feet up on a desk, apparently having a doze.

Julia smiled to herself and continued softly down the red patterned carpet and round the corner. She knew her way around the place because her grandma had lived here before she had passed away five years prior.

She pushed through the swinging door into the lounge, where a variety of sofas and easy chairs were arranged. Sunlight pooled in from the two bay windows; a large arch showing where the original divide between the two buildings had been.

There was, of all things, a full-sized pool table set in front of the nearest bay, although in all her visits Julia had never seen it being used. For that matter she had never seen the navy-blue dust cover removed from it. In the far room, Julia could see a TV warbling away to itself, the image of a politician whom she particularly disliked flickering on the screen. Thankfully, he had sent the small audience here to sleep and a white-haired couple snored loudly in front of him.

Julia led Sally over to a table in the corner where a handful of residents were sitting in front of a game of *Scrabble*. She couldn't help glancing down at the board and spotting several misspelt words which had been allowed to go unchallenged, but she reined in her instinct to point them out.

The players looked up as the women approached. A man with close-cropped white hair on the side of his head, with heavyset spectacles and a little pot belly under a chequered shirt gave Julia a smile. "Hello. Are you looking for someone in particular?" he asked.

Julia returned the smile. "Not quite. We work at the Barley Mow. We found this after the lunch shift on Sunday and thought someone here might be missing it."

Sally held out her palm to display a dangly gold earring shaped like a feather. It had been carefully selected from Sally's jewellery box to look valuable enough to be worth the effort of returning, but not so valuable that anyone would be likely to try it on for the sake of an unmatched earring.

The man leaned over the table, subtly dislodging some tiles that were paving the way to a triple word score. "I can't say I recognize it," he said. "How about you? Erin? Kendall?"

The women sat either side looked through their spectacles but agreed they didn't recognize it.

"I don't think I've seen it before, John," the first woman said.

"And we all see enough of each other around here, I'm sure we'd have noticed it at some point if it belonged to anyone here," the other said.

"Well, those of us who still have our eyesight, Kendall," the first woman remarked acidly.

"Yes, and who can still remember who they saw yesterday," Kendall added.

The two women chuckled rather mirthlessly and shot a glance at the final member of the table, a thin gentleman who had sat throughout the conversation with a toothless grin.

Julia ignored the barbed remarks and pretended to think. "You know, I thought I spotted Janice Teller with you on Sunday. Was that right? Or did I imagine that?"

"No, that would be right," John said. "The whole expedition was in honour of her grandma's ninetieth." He inclined his head at a woman in a mauve dress who was sitting in one of the chairs in the middle of the room, a book spread open on her lap. "Deborah's just over there."

"Let's check if it might be Janice's then," Sally said, giving a warm smile before turning away. "Thanks."

Julia paused before she followed her, she had one more question for the table. "We found the earring just by the back door. Do you know if Janice popped out at any point? Having a smoke, maybe?"

"Maybe," John replied. "She was out of the room for a while, if I remember."

"And why would you be paying such close attention to a young lady like that, John?" Erin asked sharply.

Kendall tapped her painted fingernails next to her *Scrabble* tiles. "I do remember her leaving the table for a while, because I was wondering if the food was disagreeing with her." She gave a smirk.

"Um, thanks," Julia said and hurried to catch Sally up. She whispered conspiratorially to her friend as they crossed the room. "We know Janice was there at least then, the vicar was right about that."

"And she disappeared for some time too," Sally added; evidently she'd caught the end of the conversation.

Julia looked meaningfully towards Janice's grandma. "Let's see if she knows if Janice left the building. If she stepped out then Janice might have told her where she was going, or at least where she was claiming to be going."

"A little underhand having her own grandma provide evidence against her," said Sally. "She looks like such a sweet old lady."

Julia's mouth formed into a tight smile. "If Janice did you-know-what then it's no less than she deserves."

Sally hummed an agreement, but she still didn't look happy about it.

They arrived in front of Julia's grandma, Deborah, and stood politely. The woman's head was bowed down towards the book in her lap, either reading or dozed off, it was hard to tell.

Sally cleared her throat but there was still no reaction.

"Excuse me Mrs–" Julia realized mid-sentence that she didn't know Janice's maiden name. "Excuse me, Deborah," she finished, raising her voice.

Still it was to no avail, the elderly lady remained apparently engrossed in her reading.

"Oi!" Sally shouted.

A few heads from around the room looked up, and Julia thought that she heard a snigger from the direction of the *Scrabble* table.

Deborah's head slowly pivoted up and she peered over the top of her glasses at them with raised eyebrows. "Yes?"

Sally held the earring out again. "We found this in the Barley Mow and were wondering if it might be your granddaughter's," she said.

The old woman adjusted her glasses, the lenses flashing as they caught the light, and inspected the earring. "Oh, yes, that's Janice's, all right," she said. With an unanticipated turn of speed, her hand came out and plucked the item from Sally's palm. "I'll pass it on to her when I see her."

Sally and Julia exchanged looks but Deborah had already turned her attention back to her book.

She spoke to the two younger women without looking up. "Was there anything else?" she asked.

"We found the earring just outside the back door. You don't know why Janice would have been out there, do you?"

Deborah gave a shrug, still not looking round. "Having a smoke, I expect. I've always maintained that it's a dreadful, dreadful habit. But she never listened to her grandma, that girl."

Julia mumbled some words of thanks and turned to go. Sally was still glaring at the earring, *her* earring, cupped tightly in Deborah's paw. Julia could see her clenching her jaw in anger and gently steered her towards the exit.

"She stole it," Sally hissed. "At least now I won't feel bad at all if she ends up having to give King's evidence against her kin."

Julia ignored her and whispered back, "I don't think I've ever once seen Janice smoke a cigarette. Whether she slipped out the back or just had a very long call of nature, I don't think we can rely on her grandmother to tell us."

Sally huffed. "Well then, I guess the old bat is a liar as well as a thief," she said.

"I'll get you a new set of earrings, Sally," Julia said, attempting to mollify her friend.

"You won't, not with your income," Sally said, but her expression softened. "Come on, we've got a killer to catch, haven't we?"

* * *

Julia noticed that Sally was looking rather thoughtful as they made their way slowly past the memorial cenotaph and back along the high street.

"Penny for your thoughts?" Julia said, breaking the silence that they had been walking in.

Sally screwed her face up and jerked her thumb over her shoulder in the direction of the care home. "Do you think we'll end up like that?"

"How do you mean?"

"All gossip and snide remarks at one another because they have nothing else to fill their time with other than a *Scrabble* game. Will that be you and me when we're old?"

Julia cast her mind back to the hours spent playing whist and rummy with Sally in the sixth form canteen in King's Barrow and thought to herself it would be more like going full circle than anything else.

Sally drifted to a halt on the pavement outside the resplendent purple frontage of Wump Wump, the little boutique shop that had opened a few years back, the latest in a long string of little boutique shops that had occupied the building, each less financially viable than the last. It was dim inside the store, and hard to see who was there, but Julia would have bet good money that it had absolutely no customers. If she had any money to bet, of course. How it kept going year to year was a mystery to her; it must be an absolute money sink.

One of the few things visible to the window-shoppers was the carved wooden jewellery case which sat under a brace of cold, white spotlights, its contents sparkling. Sally eyed them up wistfully.

"I'll get you some new earrings, Sally, even if I end up resorting to putting my hand into Donaldson's till," Julia said.

"Forget it, it's fine. I knew the risk," Sally replied, but she continued peering in the window all the same.

While her friend was occupied with window-shopping the earrings, Julia couldn't help her own gaze travelling on up the street to the old library. It was an imposing stone building, only one storey high but at the apex of its steeply slanted roof it was higher than most houses were. There was an arched stone window beside the entryway, covered up now with chipboard and looking rather dreary.

It had been built just over a hundred years before as the school rooms when Biddle was a much smaller place and then, after generations of little Biddlites had learned their letters there, it had been converted by the council into a library. That was back in the sixties when the current primary school had been erected on what was then the north edge of the village, although now it was surrounded by homes.

For half a decade Julia had worked happily in the café that sat just inside the library entrance, supplying cakes and hot drinks to the local bookworms.

For a while the extra revenue stream had been enough to keep the lights on, alongside an ever-dwindling amount of funding from the council. But in the end not even this had been enough and the library had been forced to close its doors for the last time.

Now it sat there with its chipboard cladding and an oversized cardboard sign for one of the local estate agents standing next to it, already faded from the elements. An incongruous eyesore on the otherwise picturesque village high street.

Julia sighed. She had felt totally adrift when the library had shut. Not just the loss of her steady paycheque but also the fact that the building had been a second home to her for so many years. Somewhere to go when Mum and

Dad had been arguing. A treat on the weekend to go and see what new arrivals had appeared in stock to pass a rainy day, and Somerset had plenty of those.

Julia was jarred from her thoughts and back to the present as a tractor made its slow passage up the high street towing a trailer filled with broken concrete and tiling, bouncing and rattling with every divot in the tarmac. She realized that Sally had said something to her that she hadn't registered and was now looking at her expectantly.

"Sorry?" Julia said.

"Do you want to hang around the high street all day in the hopes that Janice turns up?" Sally repeated.

"Not really."

"Because I thought maybe we could keep watch for her over at the pub."

Julia snorted. Not that Mrs Teller was entirely unknown to frequent the Barley Mow, but she wasn't exactly a regular. Still, she had heard worse ideas for ways to pass an afternoon.

When they turned off the lane and into the Barley Mow's car park, Barry was slouching against the white plaster wall of the pub next to the lone potted fir that Ivan had put out to liven up the frontage. A cigarette dangled from his hand, its smoke curling lazily up into the air.

Julia tried to catch Barry's eye as they approached over the gravel, but he obstinately refused to meet her look. Perhaps he hoped she and Sally might fail to notice him and his unscheduled smoking break if his pupils refused to look up from a particularly interesting patch of ground they'd found.

"All right, Barry," Sally shouted cheerfully as they reached the door.

Barry glanced briefly in their direction. "All right, girls," he said, raising the cigarette to his mouth.

Sally shook her head and reached for the door latch, but Julia thought she might as well try her luck.

"Hey, Barry," she said. "Do you remember if Janice Teller was here for the lunch service on Sunday?"

"Yeah, she was here," he said brusquely and puffed a cloud of smoke out around himself.

"Do you remember if she disappeared at all during the meal? Like half an hour or something like that?"

Barry scowled, eyebrows knitted together like two caterpillars colliding. "Not a clue. Why would I be paying attention to something like that?"

"I was only asking," Julia replied softly.

Barry gave a loud tut. "What do you want from me now? To wait on these people hand and foot? They only pay me minimum wage, you know?"

Sally wagged a finger at him. "You finish that fag and get inside before Ivan catches you or he won't be paying you anything. Not that I'd be too sorry to see you go," she added under her breath as she pushed at the door and stepped inside.

Julia trailed in close behind. "What an attitude," she remarked. "No wonder Mrs White got rid of him."

"Yeah, huge surprise there," Sally said, dipping her head slightly as she went under a beam. There were one or two of the regular punters in the parlour but no Mrs Teller. "So what are you having, chicken?"

Chapter 10

Mark was standing at the top of Pagan's Hill with his back turned and his hands in his jacket pockets, admiring the view. There was a large Labrador sniffing around in the undergrowth nearby. Julia had been expecting some grizzled ex-police dog so she was relieved to see that it seemed completely unthreatening, maybe even a little dopey, as it rooted around in the ferns.

At the sight of the other dog, Rumpkin bounded off up the hill, yipping excitedly. Hearing the barking terrier, Mark turned round. He was bundled up in a thick grey scarf and a woolly hat that had flopped over at the top, but still his cheeks had risen to a ruddy red colour in the cold. He gave Julia a wave as she slogged up the final section. If she was trying to impress a man, she reflected, she probably shouldn't have suggested meeting at the top of a hill. Not with her cardio level. At the very least, she should have conspired to be the first to arrive. But with her timekeeping, that was always going to be unlikely.

"Those two seem to be getting along," Mark said by way of greeting, nodding towards the dogs.

Julia watched them bounding around in circles, chasing one another, as she caught her breath. "Yes," she agreed.

"So, do you want to save some time and just run away from me now?" Mark asked.

Julia didn't deign to reply. She knew he was teasing but she didn't appreciate it.

"It's twice you've done that now," Mark added, unhelpfully.

"Yes, yes, I know. But I had good reasons."

"Did you?"

Julia cast her mind back to fleeing at the sight of Mark's dad, spilling chipolatas in her wake. "Well, I had a good reason for the second time, at least," she conceded.

"Which was?"

"Something the vicar said," Julia replied as they began to sidle along the path, cresting the hill and starting down the slope. The two dogs had disappeared into the woods on their right-hand side now, but she could still hear them crashing alongside. "Janice Teller wasn't at the morning church service on the day Mrs White was killed. So that's her alibi shot."

"Alibi? You think she did it, then?" Mark asked.

"I don't know." Julia shrugged. "She has motive enough."

"Which is?" Mark prompted.

Julia had forgotten that she had omitted certain details when she told Mark about the case. "Oh," she said. "Well, Mrs White and Mr Teller were, you know."

She gave Mark a pointed look but it was returned only by a blank one. "You know," she said again.

"Oh," Mark said. "I see."

"So Janice had motive in spades and now it seems I had her alibi all wrong. I'll keep digging, I suppose," Julia said.

Mark chuckled. "You are intent on getting to the bottom of this yourself, aren't you? You really don't have any faith in my dad."

"If it was up to him, it would still be being treated as a hit-and-run," Julia remarked.

"True enough, perhaps. Although if I remember correctly he did manage to solve a case once or twice," Mark said.

"I'm probably being uncharitable," Julia said. "But he did also give me the third degree over that death threat Mrs White received."

"The one you initially kept quiet about and then tried to phone in anonymously after it had vanished?" Mark said.

"Yes, that one," Julia muttered.

They turned off the road at this point, hopping over a low wooden stile to join a path that meandered its way in a broad circuit through the woodlands. The trees were almost bare of leaves now; they'd settled to form a crunchy carpet on the forest floor. But it was cosy enough despite the time of year, with the yellow autumn sun creating dappled patches on the ground. Julia noticed with childish satisfaction that when she breathed out heavily a little puff of steam floated away.

"I still get the feeling that there's something you're not telling me, there," Mark said, picking his way over a tangle of fallen branches. "How did you know about that note in the first place?"

Julia mulled that over. Despite her better instincts, she had to admit she liked Mark. He seemed trustworthy enough and he'd tried to chase down the red-headed man when he had fled from the Fox and Hounds. She watched as Mark's Labrador came bounding out of the woods in front of them, ran a quick circle around the pair of walkers, and disappeared back into the trees. "You're a dog-lover, aren't you, Mark?"

"I am indeed," he replied, cautiously, evidently trying to judge where Julia was going.

"Well, the reason I found that death threat was because I broke into Mrs White's office. And the reason that I broke into Mrs White's office was that she'd kidnapped my dog."

"She what?"

"You heard me. Dognapped. Rumpkin had gotten loose in the garden centre car park and she locked him in there and refused to return him unless I paid her a thousand pounds for 'lost business' or some nonsense."

Mark let out a low whistle. "That woman had a real knack for making enemies, didn't she?"

"Yes, she did. There's no end of people who might have wished her harm. But only a few people who could have stolen the major's car that morning. And yes, before you feel the need to mention it, I'm aware that I'm on that very short list of people."

Mark's dog re-emerged from the woodlands with a stick in its jaws, which he promptly deposited at his master's feet. Distractedly, Mark reached down for the stick and flung it off into the woods. "Fetch, Manny."

The stick landed with a crunch in the leaves and both dogs went bounding after it, tussling briefly for it before Manny emerged victorious and shot off with his prize. Rumpkin followed, barking at his heels.

"Wouldn't the major be your alibi?" Mark asked as he watched the dogs hare away.

"That old duffer? I don't think he'd have noticed if I spontaneously combusted at the bar. He still doesn't recognize me when I see him so I don't think I'm getting an ironclad alibi if I'm relying on him."

Mark hummed thoughtfully and they strolled along for a bit longer before Manny came bounding back for another round of fetch, dancing on his hindlegs in anticipation. Mark duly obliged and lobbed the stick again. He looked distastefully down at the palm of his hand and wiped the slobber off on his jeans.

"God, this is depressing," Julia sighed. "My whole life seems to revolve around this murder investigation now. I never seem to just have conversations about job hunting or how Mum's getting on with her new hip or anything."

Mark laughed. "Dad always liked to take his work home with him. I'm used to hearing about various cases day in and day out in lieu of an actual, meaningful conversation."

Julia shot him a sidelong glance as they walked. "Has he said anything about me?"

"A little. Not much. He still has his suspicions, I think, but for what it's worth I'm trying to talk him around."

Julia didn't know quite what to say to that. Trying to get her off the hook for murder seemed a bit above and beyond for a first date. Definitely third-date material in her book.

They clambered over another stile onto a chunk of hillside where the trees had been removed and there was scrubby meadowland with views out over the fields beyond. Just on the horizon the sea glinted in the sun. The path hugged the boundary between the meadow and the trees, a low wooden fence separating the two. Great thickets of brambles pushed their way through the fence, laden with a plentiful crop of large, lush blackberries, but it seemed that all of the berries within reach of someone of Julia's stature had already been harvested by other walkers.

Mark must have noticed Julia ignoring the panorama in front and gazing longingly at the blackberries instead, because he reached one of his long arms up and carefully picked one of the delicate fruits, offering it out to her between stained fingers.

Julia took it gingerly, popped it into her mouth and felt the juice explode out.

"It's a pity we didn't bring a bag," Julia said, thinking what wonders Sally might be able to create in the kitchen if she had a bag of these and maybe some of the windfall apples from the major's garden.

"I have something," Mark said, patting at his jacket pockets.

Wow, this is a man who comes prepared, Julia thought. Perhaps she even detected the beginnings of a swoon coming along.

His face beaming with pride, Mark produced with a flourish a thin plastic bag from his breast pocket. Julia started to reach for it but then paused, with her fingers hovering.

"That's a dog-poo bag," she said.

"Don't worry, it's not been used or anything, it'll be fine," Mark said.

"Ew. No. The blackberries would be all pooey." Julia scrunched up her face.

Mark shook his head at her. "Suit yourself."

By this time they were nearing the kissing gate that led back into the woods. "Pick me another one, would you?" she said.

Mark obliged, reaching up again and passing her a second blackberry.

Julia's heart beat slightly faster as she wriggled her way through the kissing gate, wondering if Mark might try to steal a peck on the cheek as they navigated their way through, but despite his juvenile sense of humour he didn't give it a try.

"So, what do you do for a living?" Mark asked.

"I don't," Julia replied.

"Hm?"

"I don't do anything for a living. Not since the library in Biddle Rhyne closed down. I used to work in the café there. Now I only work the odd shift at Mr Donaldson's place or the Barley Mow. But mostly I just draw my savings down and rack up my credit card."

Julia was painfully aware that she wasn't exactly making herself sound like a catch but her mum had always taught her honesty was the best policy. If there were going to be more dates, then Mark was going to realize the truth sooner or later. "One day the bailiffs will come and repossess all my stuff but the joke will be on them, it's all completely worthless."

"The library makes sense for you, given how you were waxing lyrical about books in the Fox and Hounds."

"Wine has that effect on me," Julia said.

They walked along a bit further, the sound of the dogs crashing along among the trees somewhere behind them.

"And what do you do for a living?" she asked Mark.

"Oh. I'm a copper, like my old man. I only came along here to pump you for information," Mark said casually.

Julia didn't need to look round to know that he had one of his stupid ear-to-ear grins splitting his face.

"What do you really do?" she asked.

"I'm a painter."

"The arty kind?" Julia said.

"No, the boring kind that paints walls."

"Useful, though. You never know when you need someone to paint a wall for you," Julia said.

When they were almost at the point where the track emerged back onto the road, Mark said, "I guess this is about where we part ways." Julia saw him grinning and knew that a dig was coming her way. "Will there be a second date? Or do you want to sprint away from me into the distance with no explanation?"

Julia allowed herself a small smile this time. "There could be a second date, I think. Coffee? Monday?"

"Your place?"

"Good try. Don't you dare ask your dad for the address. How about the café on Biddle High Street? I'll give you my number."

Chapter 11

Milk, News & More was a small convenience store just off Biddle's high street, more commonly known simply as Donaldson's after its mercurial proprietor.

Outside, the façade of the old Victorian end-terrace had been covered over in garishly coloured, oversized pictures of the produce on sale inside. Thus it was that someone walking up from the village green would be presented with eight foot tall photos of milk bottles, newspapers, bread, canned tomatoes and dog food just before they reached the high street. When it had opened its doors for the first time a decade earlier, the genteel residents of Biddle Rhyne had derided it as a complete affront to the rural ambience of their village and then promptly flocked there in their droves to pick up any bits and pieces they had neglected in their weekly shop.

The inside of the building was just as uninspiring as the outside. The original walls had been covered over with smooth magnolia plasterwork, and even most of this was hidden by shelf upon shelf of packaged produce with another floor-to-ceiling shelf bisecting the space into two cramped aisles. At the counter next to the door, Julia stood in front of the regulation-grey sliding cabinet for tobacco products. She was wearing a polo shirt of scarlet with blue triangles, which she'd changed into after her walk with Mark. In theory these were the store colours, as had been explained to her when she started, but even the illuminated sign that spanned the entrance outside didn't match. Still, Mr Donaldson insisted that it be worn.

She drummed her fingers idly on the one section of the counter that was free of merchandise, where the store's card-payment policy was displayed, trapped under a thick sheet of Perspex. She'd long ago learned that time had little meaning here in Donaldson's and passed with all the speed of treacle. Surreptitiously, Julia snuck her phone from her jeans pocket and checked for messages. Donaldson had caught her doing this once early on in her tenure and given her such an earful that now she always double-checked she was alone in the shop before doing so.

The door swung open, the scuffing sound it made along the floor tiles alerting her before the bell gave out its dull jangle, and she stuffed the phone away quickly and looked up attentively, but it was only Mrs Singh and Mrs Trevcock. Julia just about managed to give the two customers a welcoming smile but they were too deep in conversation to notice, chattering away to each other as they disappeared from view behind the central shelf.

"You heard about what happened to poor, dear Audrey White, I assume?" Julia heard Mrs Singh saying.

"Oh, I did. Just the most awful news. I've always said the police should crack down on the boy racers that go round those country lanes. And to not come forward after it? The things some people do," Mrs Trevcock replied, tutting at several points in her speech.

Mrs Singh lowered her voice, although she was still clearly audible through the canned pineapples. "I heard that it might not be an accident after all. That maybe Mrs White was hit on purpose."

"No!" Julia heard Mrs Trevcock gasp.

At that point the bell over the door rang again. Julia managed to tear her eyes from the shelf concealing the two women. Mr Pegg stepped in, gave Julia a cheery wave and went to browse the magazine rack.

Julia turned her attention back to the conversation on the other side of the central shelf.

"Oh, yes," said Mrs Singh's voice. "My Kev said one of the staff at the Barley Mow has a grudge with Audrey. Someone saw the two of them arguing with each other hammer and tongs a couple of weeks ago. And they'd have had the chance to take that silly old major's car, too."

"No. I don't believe it. Everyone at that pub's so sweet. They practically moved heaven and earth for us when it was our anniversary. So who was it then?"

A fishing magazine landed on the counter with a slap, a hapless-looking carp staring up from the glossy cover.

Mr Pegg slid a five-pound note over the counter towards Julia. "Just this and one of the number-five scratch cards please, Julia," he said chirpily.

"Shh!" Julia raised her finger to her lips, and craned forward to try and catch Mrs Singh's reply.

Mr Pegg looked round over his shoulders at the apparently innocuous view of Donaldson's store and then back to Julia with a perplexed expression.

"Oh, I don't think I should say," came Mrs Singh's voice.

"What's the matter?" Mr Pegg asked.

"I said 'Sh!'. This could be important," Julia said.

"I just wanted—" Mr Pegg began.

Julia snorted angrily from her nostrils. "Fine," she snapped, snatching the five-pound note up and ringing it through the till as quickly as she could manage. "Take your magazine." She made a shooing gesture with her fingers.

"There was also…" Mr Pegg said, but he read the expression on Julia's face and slunk away.

Luckily, Mrs Trevcock was still exhorting her friend to spill the beans.

"Okay, I really shouldn't be telling you this. But…" Mrs Singh's voice dropped a few decibels in deference to the sensitive nature of the revelation she was about to make, and Julia had to lean forward on her stomach across the countertop in order to keep listening.

"I heard it was that Julia Ford. Apparently she let that mutt of hers run all around the garden centre barking and yipping at customers and scaring children until eventually dear little Audrey had to ask her to put it on a lead. The things that Julia said to her, they would make a sailor blush."

Behind the counter, Julia suppressed a growl and bit down on her bottom lip in order to prevent herself giving the old gossip a few choice words of her own to think about.

"Well, well," Mrs Trevcock said. "I can't say I'm all that surprised. There was always something a bit off about that girl."

Julia's mouth swung open. All restraint was gone now and she would have given the old trout both barrels if she hadn't been too apoplectic to form words.

"Where did your Kev hear all this from?" Mrs Trevcock asked.

"Oh, his name escapes me. You know that nice young lad who works at the Barley Mow?" Mrs Singh said.

Julia's rage had subsided fractionally now and she took a deep, calming breath. She couldn't think who answered that description though.

"You mean Barry?" Mrs Trevcock suggested.

She couldn't have meant Barry, he was in no way a nice young lad, as anyone with functioning eyes, ears or nose would have known.

"Yes, that's right, young Barry. Kev popped into the Barely Mow the other day to ask if Barry still had that bicycle to sell and the two of them got chatting. You know what a gossip Kev can be when he wants to."

The two women rounded the corner of the aisle, a single pint of milk nestling in the plastic basket apparently the sole result of their extended shop. Mrs Singh trundled smiling up to the counter, without a hint of shame on her wrinkled face, and put the basket down.

"Hello there, dear," Mrs Singh trilled.

Julia cleared her throat long and hard; unable to meet the old woman's eyes, she glared down at the milk with a face of thunder. "Is that everything, Mrs Singh?" Julia's voice came out forced and raspy.

"That's everything," Mrs Singh replied, carefully counting twenty-pence pieces out of her purse and stacking them on the counter. She picked the milk bottle up and gave a little wave with her fingers before linking arms with Mrs Trevcock and heading out of the shop.

Just as the door was closing, Mrs Singh leaned into her friend and Julia just caught her say, "You see? I told you she was an odd one, didn't I?"

Julia stood smouldering for some time, watching the pile of silvers like they might suddenly try to leap up and bite. Eventually she swept them smartly from the glass countertop with one palm and deposited them into the till with the other.

So that was the version of events about her and Mrs White that was circulating the village, was it? And perhaps more to the point, that was the version of events that Barry had been circulating, the nice young lad, as he pedalled about on his bicycle.

A thought began forming at the back of Julia's mind and began trying to elbow forwards, pushing aside the more numerous angry thoughts that were currently occupying Julia's attention.

A bicycle. If Barry had a bicycle then he could get down the side of Pagan's Hill right quick. Her earlier time trial hadn't proved anything. All she'd done was waste her morning marching up and down the lane. She balled her hands up into fists. What an idiot she'd been. This sleuthing business was harder than she'd thought. She would think it was best left to the professionals, if the professionals of the area weren't represented by that great fool of an inspector.

Julia yanked her phone back out of her pocket, called up the Barley Mow and held it up to her ear while it rang for an intolerably long time.

Eventually a voice answered on the other end. "Barley Mow. Barry speaking."

"Barry," Julia hissed. Now was not the time to take him to task, she needed information. "I need to speak to Sally, it's urgent."

"Sorry, Ivan says no personal calls," he replied.

"It's not a personal call, it's... about shifts," Julia said.

There was a quiet beep from the phone and with rising anger Julia realized that Barry had hung up on her. She glanced quickly at the clock. Still fifteen minutes until closing. She paced restlessly up and down the aisle a couple of times. It wasn't like there were any customers, anyway. She stepped onto the pavement and then, stretching as far as she could manage, got her fingertips onto the shutters and pulled them down. A few minutes later she was marching down the street in the direction of the Barley Mow.

A light, mizzling rain started to drift down just as she turned onto the lane. The foldout umbrella from her handbag did little to stop it soaking her through and when she finally stomped into the parlour, Julia was wet and irritable.

Sally looked up from behind the bar, surprised to see her. "Have you come straight from work?" she asked.

Julia looked down at the less-than-flattering colours of her work shirt, not much improved for being darkened by the rain that was now being flicked onto the window panes as the wind picked up. She ignored the question, deeming it stupid, and leaned across the top of the bar to talk in a low voice to her friend, checking that Barry was nowhere in sight as she did so.

"Did you know that Barry had a bike?" Julia asked.

"Oh, yeah. He rode it here on his very first shift. But he arrived in such a sweaty mess from hauling himself up Pagan's Hill that Ivan forbade him from using it again."

"Right. But if he did run Mrs White down, then he could have had his bicycle stashed somewhere nearby and rode it back to the pub. So he could have been back way quicker than I walked it the other day."

Sally bit her bottom lip thoughtfully. "You would have noticed if he had arrived back all sweaty and out of breath, though, wouldn't you?"

"That's just it, though. He would have already been near the top of the hill, he would only have had to freewheel it down again. Even Barry wouldn't have worked up a sweat doing that and it would still have been twice as fast as I could walk."

"Hm. I guess you're right. And there's more, too."

"What?"

Sally had a quick look over her shoulder to make sure that they weren't being overhead. "I spoke to some of the kitchen staff today. They said none of them saw Barry when they took their smoke breaks. He disappeared somewhere all right, but he wasn't out in the smoking area."

At that point, the door from the dining area swung open and Barry slouched in, loosely holding an empty tray by his side.

Sally and Julia quickly pulled away from each other and tried to look casual. Julia rested one elbow on the bar and pretended to be very interested in the specials board that hung on the far wall.

Barry stood for a moment, eyeing the two women before disappearing through into the kitchen. Julia watched him go.

"We'd better keep an eye on him, he's up to something," Sally whispered.

Julia nodded in agreement.

* * *

When Julia got home from letting Rumpkin lift his leg, Sally was sitting in the kitchen, perched on one of the pair of faux-leather-topped breakfast stools. She was still wearing her black work outfit so apparently she hadn't been home long. She was also wearing a peculiar expression on her face. Whimsical with a hint of smugness. She obviously knew something that Julia didn't.

Julia steeled herself for the worst. "What is it?" she asked, her eyes narrow with suspicion as she slung her handbag down onto the countertop.

"Mark was in the Barley Mow after you left," said Sally, her voice playful and teasing.

"Oh?" Julia tried to seem nonchalant. She thought she stood a decent enough chance of getting through the exchange without blushing like a schoolgirl at any point, although she wasn't sure that she could hope for any better than that.

"Yes. He was looking for you. He left you something." Sally's mischievous blue eyes flickered to the far countertop by the hob. There was a little gift-wrapped box there, about six inches across.

Julia crossed the laminate floor to the mystery box and reached for it, aware that Sally had pivoted around on her stool to watch. Julia peeled the paper apart trying not to seem too eager.

Inside was a sealed plastic box. Nothing fancy, the kind you might acquire free after a takeaway.

"Open it, then," Sally hissed, giving up her pretence of being a neutral observer in the affair.

Julia popped the lid. Inside, the box was packed full with blackberries. Most of them looked perfect, evidently hand-chosen to impress, although a few had met sad demises during their travels and coated their companions in sticky purple juice. Julia's heart melted at the sight of them.

"Blackberries?" Sally squawked, and looked askance at her friend. "Why blackberries?"

Julia didn't reply, but stood and happily admired the little gift Mark had provided.

"They do look nice, though," Sally said, her fingers reaching out towards the box.

Julia slapped them away. "They're not for eating," she said hastily.

Sally looked hurt and rubbed her hand, despite the slap being rather a gentle one. "Well, what are they for, then? Are you going to put little pins in them and display them like a butterfly collection?"

"They're for cooking with," Julia replied merrily.

"Are you sure, Julia? They look like pretty decent blackberries and I don't think I can stand idly by and let you cremate them."

Briefly, memories floated into Julia's mind, memories of smoke-filled kitchens and hours spent at the sink scouring the charred remains of food from ruined baking trays and Pyrex dishes.

"Well, maybe you should do the actual cooking," she replied.

"After you just slapped my hand? Not very likely," Sally said.

Chapter 12

It's a good plan, Julia thought, even if Rumpkin doesn't agree.

She was sitting stationary in the car halfway up Pagan's Hill, the entrance for Forge Lane just ahead of her. Janice Teller should be rounding the corner any minute, on her way to play the organ at the church, and Julia was planning to 'coincidentally' bump into her on her way to walk the dog.

Rumpkin, however, couldn't understand why he'd been bundled into the car only to be kept in the boot. His initial excitement at going on a car ride had petered out and now he sat with his head resting on the top of back seats, looking forlorn.

Julia did her best to ignore his occasional whine and keep focused on Forge Lane. It was important that Janice didn't spot her lurking about. Julia needed to catch her with her guard down.

Someone rounded the bend and Julia sat up, alert, and craned forward towards the windscreen. It was definitely Janice, dressed in a neat red cardigan and black trousers. Julia put the car into gear and started to drive slowly up the hill.

The road was narrow at this point and Janice squeezed aside to make way for the car, pushing her back against the hedge. But instead of passing by, Julia pulled up alongside her. It was a mean trick to play, practically trapping the woman between the car and the hedge, but Julia felt her extreme methods were justified.

Julia wound the window down and stuck her head out. "Oh, hi, Janice," she called. "Nice weather, isn't it?"

Julia gave a smile, doing her best to appear casual. But she needn't have made the effort. Janice was visibly distracted, staring off into space, and it was only when she heard her name that she bothered to glance at the car and its driver.

"Hello, um, Julia," Janice said. "Yes, it turned out nice."

"You know, I thought I saw you eating at the pub the other day when I was working," Julia said, her voice still cheerful and upbeat.

Janice's head bobbed in a little nod.

There didn't seem to be anything more forthcoming, so Julia continued. "I went looking for you when I was on my break, but I couldn't find you," she said. "Did you pop out?"

If Janice had been distracted before then those words sharpened her focus. Her crystal-blue eyes widened and looked straight at Julia. "What? No, I didn't go anywhere. You could ask my gran. I was there the whole time."

Julia kept her easy smile fixed in place, but inwardly she felt her suspicions growing. Janice was lying to her. At least if the residents at the care home were to be believed, Janice had gone missing for some time during the meal.

"Really?" said Julia. "Because I spent a bit of time looking—"

Before she could interrogate Janice any further, Julia was interrupted by the sound of a car horn close behind her, making her jump in the seat. She'd been so fixated on

Janice that she hadn't even heard the other vehicle coming up the hill.

Looking in the wing mirror, she could see the radiator grille of a large truck filling the lane.

Julia thought quickly, trying to work out how to avoid Janice wriggling off the hook, but a second later one of the truck doors slammed and a figure was marching towards her up the lane.

She swallowed as Lance's large frame appeared at her window, looming over her as he brought his head down so they were almost nose to nose.

"Lance…" Julia began, but he thundered over the top of her.

"I thought I told you to leave us alone?" he shouted, the colour rising in his face.

Julia instinctively shrank back into the car. In the boot, Rumpkin began to bark excitedly.

"I was just taking the dog for a walk," Julia said, suddenly finding it surprisingly hard to get words out. Lance had a way of unnerving her even when he wasn't bellowing at her.

Lance's scowl turned briefly onto Rumpkin before aiming itself at Julia again. "Don't take me for a fool," he said. He wasn't shouting anymore, his voice was low and even now, but that was somehow much worse. "You mind your own business or you'll regret it."

With that, Lance straightened up and stalked back to his van.

Janice's eyes shot from her husband to Julia. "You'd better believe him," she whispered. "You don't really know what he's capable of."

Julia couldn't tell if that was a threat or a warning, but before she could reply, Janice had squeezed past the side of her car, branches rustling as she pushed through them, and was hurrying away downhill.

Acutely aware of Lance behind her, Julia started the car again and pulled off. There was a jerk, and in her haste to leave she stalled the car. Muttering at herself under her breath, Julia turned the key and tried again, the engine protesting as she clamped her foot down on the accelerator.

She watched in the mirrors and offered a quiet prayer of thanks as Lance's truck turned off up Forge Lane towards his home.

Rumpkin was barking furiously. It was somehow reassuring.

"You'd have protected me, wouldn't you, boy?" Julia said.

Rumpkin barked once more before falling silent. Julia couldn't help but smile. She could feel her heart starting to slow down a bit.

"Come on, we'd better give you a walk before you pop, hadn't we?" she said.

* * *

The stick thudded to the ground sending dried brown leaves floating up from the spot where it had landed. The stick's arrival was shortly followed by Rumpkin, churning up more of the leaf mould as he scampered across the forest floor, all four paws scrambling for purchase as he yipped along excitedly.

He snatched the bit of tree branch up into his jaws and bounded back to his mistress who was making her way idly down the curving path. He opened his mouth to let the stick fall at Julia's feet and looked up at her with expectant eyes.

"Sorry, boy, the game ends here," Julia said. She patted him roughly behind the ears before clipping the fabric lead on to the ring on his collar.

Despite his enthusiasm for the game, Rumpkin accepted this meekly and trotted obediently at Julia's heels as she opened the little kissing gate that led back onto the lane.

She was just about to cross the road, back to where she had parked up the car, when a bell started to ping frantically further up the lane. She turned around to see a bright red bicycle careening downhill towards her, the Lycra-clad rider waving their arms frantically.

"Quick! Quick! Get out of the way, I can't stop!" the rider warbled as they ploughed onwards.

Julia jumped back, pressing herself flat against the gate and giving a sharp jerk on the lead to bring Rumpkin close to heel beside her.

She wasn't a moment too soon; the bike whizzed past, missing Rumpkin's snout by mere inches.

Julia watched the out-of-control vehicle as it continued on its way, serpentining across the narrow lane as it went, accompanied by a high-pitched shout from its rider.

It didn't get very far. Just down the road was a sharp bend, too sharp for the bike to take at its rather considerable speed. Despite their best efforts, the cyclist made it halfway around the bend and then the bike upended itself in spectacular fashion, throwing the rider from the handlebars. Mercifully they landed in a drift of autumn leaves that had banked up at the corner while the bike fared less well and collided solidly with the sprawling oak tree which grew at the roadside.

Julia began to jog downhill to the scene of the crash to see if she could help, with Rumpkin running and barking alongside.

By the time she reached the rider he was sitting upright in the pile of leaves, looking a bit dazed and rubbing his elbows which appeared to have taken the brunt of the fall.

"Are you all right?" Julia gasped, coming to a halt at the edge of the road.

"Oh. Battered and bruised. What a nasty fall. I think I'll probably live, though," came the reply.

Julia recognized the nasal voice before she had a chance to see the cyclist's face properly, there was no mistaking Mr Smedley, the newly promoted garden centre premier.

He plucked his glasses from the leaves beside him and carefully placed them back on before straightening up his helmet which had been sitting rather askew on top of his head. He craned his face up to look at Julia, shielding his eyes from the sun, low in the sky at this time of year.

"Ah, Julia Ford. Sorry about that, the bike rather got away from me," Mr Smedley said.

"That's quite all right. Are you sure you're okay? You took quite a tumble," Julia said.

Mr Smedley looked down at red patches on his elbows where they had been scraped raw in the fall. "Yes, I've had worse, I think."

He began to scramble awkwardly to his feet and Julia tentatively reached out a hand to help him. He was dressed from head to toe in cycling gear: a sleek helmet, luminescent Lycra T-shirt and shorts. Julia quickly averted her eyes from the prominent bulge in the skin-tight crotch of his cycling shorts. Although it had all picked up a few scuffs and snags in the fall he'd just suffered, all the gear was obviously so new that it might as well have still had the store tags attached to it.

"I didn't know that you cycled," Julia said.

Mr Smedley glanced down at where the bike had come to a premature halt against the tree. "Yes, well." He cleared his throat and did his best to smooth the creased Lycra back into place. "Young Barry sold me this contraption shortly after he was let go. I only bought it because I felt a bit sorry for him and wanted to help him out. But I thought it would be a good excuse to get me into shape. Being deputy manager of a big place like Only Gardens doesn't leave a lot of free time, unfortunately. Well, manager now, I suppose I should rightfully say."

Mr Smedley began walking stiffly over towards his bicycle. Julia gave Rumpkin's lead a little tug and followed him.

"You said that you bought the bike from Barry?" Julia asked.

"Mmhmm," Mr Smedley hummed in agreement.

"When was that? Do you remember?"

"Oh. I think it was about a fortnight after Mrs White, God rest her, let him go from Only Gardens. He found some work at a pub shortly after and I ran into him there, which was rather an awkward encounter, I must say. He didn't seem overly thrilled at his change of employment and apparently the landlord there had something against him cycling to work. So I agreed to take it off his hands. Two hundred and fifty pounds I gave him."

Julia's mind whirled through the calendar. Two weeks after Barry was let go from the garden centre. That was well before Mrs White had been run down so it seemed unlikely that Barry would have cycled away from the crime scene and back to the Barley Mow. Still, he'd been acting incredibly shifty recently; he was hiding something and she was sure about that. She just needed to get to the bottom of what it was.

They reached the spot where the bike lay rather forlornly at the side of the road and both peered down at it. The front wheel was dented in where it had collided with the tree trunk, and as Mr Smedley hauled the bike upright, Julia saw that the paint was scratched off in a couple of places in long, grey streaks. Even looking past this, though, it was obvious that the clunky old thing was not worth anywhere near the two hundred and fifty pounds that Mr Smedley had paid for it. Julia was no cyclist, but she'd count herself lucky if she could offload it for a tenner on Gumtree. Mr Smedley was no fool. Beneath his no-nonsense, businesslike appearance, he must have a bleeding heart if he was willing to give Barry that amount of cash for the thing.

Mr Smedley gave the bicycle a visual appraisal and spun the misshapen wheel with one of his hands, cocking his head to listen to the unhealthy clacking sound it made as it rotated.

"Well, I don't think this is going to get me home again," Mr Smedley said.

"No, I don't think so either." Julia agreed as she watched the wheel grind to a halt. "I can give you a lift home, if you like. I'm only parked up the road."

"Do you think we'll get the bike into the boot?" Mr Smedley asked.

Julia made a quick mental estimate. "I'd expect so." Rumpkin would have to ride in the back seats but that would be the highlight of the day as far as he was concerned. Even after seeing a cyclist upend himself into a leaf pile.

Mr Smedley stroked his chin. "Perhaps you could give me a lift down to the Barley Mow instead? If our Barry is working there I wonder if he might want the bike back again. No cash needed. To be honest, I'm not convinced that cycling is really for me."

Julia smiled to herself as they walked back uphill towards the car, Mr Smedley lifting the broken front wheel from the ground and pushing the bike along on its back wheel.

"Actually, Julia, there was something else," Mr Smedley said.

"What's that?"

"I was going through some of the accounts at Only Gardens."

"Yes?"

"There's no record of you doing any window cleaning. No invoices, no receipts."

"Oh," Julia said.

"I don't like to believe that Mrs White would be party to such cash-in-hand work, so the obvious explanation of course is that the paperwork was misplaced at some point."

"Yes," Julia agreed. "That's probably it."

Mr Smedley continued. "All the same, I will have to ask that you return the five pounds that I gave you for your services the other day. Unless you're able to produce the correct paperwork for your agreement."

They reached the car and Julia stopped and turned to face him. If Mr Smedley looked uncomfortable then he didn't show it in the slightest.

Julia sighed and opened her handbag. She rooted around for some time and eventually found enough loose pound coins to make up the required amount and placed it into Mr Smedley's waiting palm.

"Thank you," Mr Smedley said. He patted around at his Lycra cycling shorts before realizing that he had no pockets to speak of and closed his fingers awkwardly around the loose change instead.

Between them, Julia and Mr Smedley managed to take the wheel off the bicycle and jimmy it into the boot of the car while Rumpkin sat back, supervising the operation.

Mr Smedley gave a small nod of satisfaction as they finally managed to pull the boot door shut and he gave it a quick pat.

"You know what? I may as well walk back from here and save you the trouble of driving me home. If you'd be good enough to return the bicycle to Barry."

Julia folded her arms across her chest and scowled. Assuming that Barry even wanted the half-mangled bicycle back again. Otherwise she was lumped with the useless piece of junk.

Mr Smedley gave a little wave, a pound coin spilling unnoticed from his hand as he did so. "Goodbye, Julia. I'll be seeing you around, I'm sure." And with that he turned and started walking smartly up the hill, his padded Lycra shorts squeaking as he went.

Julia opened the passenger side door for Rumpkin. "Come on then, in you get. At least you'll enjoy the ride, won't you? Maybe you can be the one to explain to Sally why the front of the car is covered in dog hair."

Rumpkin woofed and sprang lithely into the front seat.

* * *

Julia pulled up on the gravel underneath the swinging sign for the Barley Mow and ratcheted the handbrake on. The evening was drawing in now and the row of spotlights at the top of the sign flickered into life, lighting up the cheery golden picture of a barley sheaf.

After a bit of effort she managed to manhandle Mr Smedley's bike out of the boot of the car and she rested it against one of the chain-linked bollards that separated the grounds of the pub from the lane. She considered briefly if she needed to locate a bike lock, but looking at the mangled bit of kit she decided it was unlikely that it was going to get nicked, even given Biddle Rhyne's rather worrying recent crime spree.

She crunched over the gravel, Rumpkin padding quickly ahead of her and pulling her along by the lead.

Inside, Sally stood behind the bar, leaning on it with one elbow, looking a trifle bored. The parlour was quiet: the major sat dozing behind his broadsheet and there was a young couple she didn't recognize on a table in the far corner. But judging by the number of cars parked round the side of the pub there was decent trade going on in the dining room.

"Is Barry around?" Julia asked, after exchanging greetings with Sally.

Her friend looked down at the tray on the bar next to her, fully laden with an assortment of drinks, beads of perspiration sliding slowly down them and forming a puddle. "He is working today, although I use that term loosely," Sally said. "He's disappeared off somewhere, I haven't seen him in ages. You could go round back and look for him, if you like."

Julia hesitated. "I'm not sure that I should. I'm not officially an employee. What would Ivan make of it?"

"Frankly, you'd be doing me a favour if you go and find Barry. If you run into Ivan just tell him that I sent you looking for that shiftless layabout and I doubt it will be you or me who gets in trouble from it."

"Okay," Julia said, still a little unsure. "Can you keep an eye on Rumpkin?"

"Of course."

Julia slipped the lead from Rumpkin's collar and the dog trundled happily off towards the spitting logs on the fire.

Sally lifted up the hinge in the bar and Julia pattered through, still unable to shake the feeling that she was doing something a bit untoward.

As she passed her, Sally put a hand gently on Julia's forearm. "Are you going sleuthing?" she asked her, keeping her voice low.

Julia nodded. "Yes. No. Sort of. Apparently Barry had already sold his bike by the time Mrs White was killed. So it seems he didn't cycle away from the scene of the crime at any rate. I'm here to make enquiries if he wants his bike back again, but I'll see if I can get anything out of him about where he disappeared to that day. He had to be somewhere after all."

"Good luck," Sally said.

Julia pushed open the door behind the bar. There was a small labyrinth of corridors here that split off in all directions. Apparently the previous generations of owners hadn't been much for forward planning and every extension the bar had accumulated over the centuries had resulted in a new twist or turn, usually involving a small flight of steps or a woefully undersized door that even Julia needed to duck to get through. Glancing through the glass in the doors ahead, she could see that Barry wasn't in the kitchen, and besides, the staff there would have moved him along rather than let him stay there underfoot for too long.

After a bit of deliberation, Julia headed through into the walk-in fridge next to the swing doors for the kitchen, figuring it would be best bet for mooching around undisturbed until Ivan rooted him out.

Her instincts didn't let her down, she pushed the heavy door with a grunt of effort and as it opened there was a flurry of movement in the fridge and she was just in time to see someone disappearing behind one of the shelves.

"Barry?" Julia called.

There was no answer so she proceeded on into the chill room, poking her head round the side of the shelves where she'd seen the movement. And sure enough there was Barry, looking very studiously at a box of pre-packaged desserts.

"Barry," Julia repeated, standing not two feet from him now.

He turned from the desserts, affecting to notice Julia for the first time although it was painfully clear that he was putting it on. He twisted his mouth into a surprised 'O' shape. "What are you doing here?" he asked, not in a belligerent way but certainly he didn't seem happy to see her.

"Well, for one thing, Sally sent me in to find out where you'd got to. There's a drinks order that's sitting on the bar ready to go," Julia said.

"Yes, well, I was just checking on the, um…" Barry trailed off and tapped the box of desserts a couple of times.

Julia rolled her eyes. "And now that I've found you, Mr Smedley was wondering if you'd like your bike back. Free of charge. He says it isn't for him. It might need a new front wheel, though."

Barry snorted. "Not sure what use a bike is without a front wheel but okay, I could probably be persuaded to take the bike back."

Just as Julia was about to roll her eyes for a second time there was the sound of a footstep directly behind her, making her jump.

She spun quickly around but the person, whoever it was, was disappearing through the doorway out of the refrigerator, and she only caught the sight of the heel of their shoe.

"Who was that?" Julia gasped, her heart fluttering from the fright. There was only the one door, they must have been lurking in the fridge with them the whole time.

"Who was what?" Barry asked.

Julia stared at him like he was mad. From where he was standing he must have had a full view of whoever had just fled out of the fridge.

"The person who just bolted out the door," Julia snapped.

"I didn't see anyone," Barry said.

Julia gave a growl of exasperation and rushed from the fridge as fast as she could; if she was lucky, she'd still catch the person.

She emerged back into the corridors in time to see the rear door of the pub swinging shut and she pounded down the narrow passageway towards it.

"Wait!" Barry called after her, leaning out of the walk-in fridge. "That's staff only."

Julia ignored him and carried on her pursuit, wrenching the small wooden door open again and slipping outside. Dusk had settled in quickly and there were no lights round the back of the pub, save for what was spilling out from the open doorway and the kitchen windows. Empty beer and cider casks were piled up to Julia's right and a hastily erected wooden bin store to her left hid the big metal wheelie bins. Above them the extractor fans from the kitchen whirred noisily as they blew big clouds of steam out into the evening air.

Julia strained to hear over the sound of the fans, and just picked out the sound of someone crunching their way across the gravel towards the car park. She started off again, as quickly as she dared in the failing light, but just as she reached the car park an engine churned into life and all she saw was the twin red tail lights of a car peeling away, sending a shower of small stones up behind them in their haste.

She stood for a moment or two with her hands on her hips, catching her breath and watching the car wind its way rapidly up the lane towards the village and out of sight. She hadn't managed to glimpse anything that would give her an inkling who she had just been chasing, and it seemed Barry was not going to be forthcoming about whoever he had been conspiring with in the fridge.

Angry and defeated, Julia made her way back past the bin store to find that the door had been shut behind her. She tugged at the iron handle although she knew it would lock on its own. "Barry," she hissed; she was certain she'd left it open when she'd made her way through.

She stormed round to the front of the pub and back in through the parlour door. Rumpkin woofed a greeting at her from a corner of the room but she ignored him and went up to Sally at the bar.

The tray of drinks had gone, finally, so it seemed Barry had been in.

"What's the matter?" Sally asked, reading the anger on Julia's features.

"There was someone in the fridge with Barry," Julia said, clambering up onto one of the stools.

"Huh? One of the staff?" said Sally.

"No. I don't think so. I didn't see them but they just legged it out the back and drove off."

"How strange. Did you ask Barry who it was?"

"Yes," Julia said. "But he's playing dumb."

"He's good at that," Sally observed drily.

Julia wasn't in the mood to smile. "Get me a wine, would you?"

"Aren't you driving?" Sally asked.

Julia grunted. "Then get me... get me some flipping answers from Barry. Wring them out of him if you have to."

"Don't worry, chicken," Sally said, producing a bottle of fruit juice from behind the bar. "We'll get to the bottom of it, you'll see."

Chapter 13

The imaginatively named Coffee on the High Street was a small coffee shop on, surprisingly enough, Biddle Rhyne's high street.

It was one of the few modern buildings on the road, sandwiched in between two much older and grander buildings; one was still residential, although subdivided up into flats, and the other was a solicitor's office. Drawing up wills was, ironically enough, the lifeblood of Biddle's economy.

The café's floor-to-ceiling windows were enlivened by decals of stylized silhouettes of steaming coffee mugs and their little chalk sandwich board stood on the narrow pavement, displaying the day's specials and generally blocking the passage of Biddle's pedestrians. Which is one way to get people to window-shop, Julia supposed.

She sat perched on one of the high stools with her back to the door, enjoying the aroma of coffee that pervaded the building. Mark had disappeared around the corner to the counter some time ago. Presumably there was a queue, certainly the place was beginning to pack in now. Lunchtime was fast approaching and the café benefitted from being one of the few places in Biddle to serve food. Or anything at all, for that matter.

At long last, Mark reappeared bearing a saucer in each hand, and on each saucer was a tall white mug, contents sloshing perilously as he walked. Julia thanked him as she reached up to take the one offered to her, carefully lowering it down to the dazzling metal table.

She hadn't specified a size, but it seemed that her date hadn't wanted to appear in anyway cheap because he'd defaulted to the largest one on the menu and now she had a latte that was just about big enough that she could disrobe and have a swim around in it, if the fancy took her at any point.

Julia lifted the coffee to her lips, burnt them slightly, and returned the mug to its saucer. Mark didn't appear to have the same problem because he took a long drink from his, wiping away the foamy moustache it left behind with the back of his hand.

"Thanks for this," Julia said, indicating the coffee with a nod of her head. "And thanks for the blackberries as well."

"You're very welcome," Mark replied. "I hope you made something nice out of them."

"Well, Sally did," Julia said.

"Ah. She's the chef of the household, is she?"

"She is indeed. I'm not much use in the kitchen unless the food has microwave instructions printed on. Now, out of you and your dad I'm guessing that you're the cook."

"Oh, my dad can cook," Mark said.

"I underestimated him, then," Julia said.

Mark flashed his teeth. "A dangerous mistake. He can make a call to the Indian. He can make a call to the Chinese."

"Ah." Julia put her elbow on the table and rested her chin on her fist. She stared dreamily up at the ceiling. "How nice it must be to live somewhere metropolitan like King's Barrow where you have all the world's cuisine available to you like that."

Mark laughed. "But, yes, I can cook when I put my mind to it. And when I find the time."

"Speaking of food, did you want to order something here? It might not be the Michelin-starred fine dining that you townsfolk are used to. But it's simple, honest fare, like the people here." Julia deliberately thickened her always rather transient West Country accent.

Mark glanced down at the time on his phone. "Better not. The queue here's insane and I'll need to be back at the site in half an hour or so."

"Oh, yes, 'work'. I dimly remember that as something that people do." Julia swilled her coffee around in its oversized mug, watching the foam go around, changing colour as it did so. Unemployed and unable to cook. She was not doing so well at this whole dating thing. She might as well have set Mark up with Sally and be done with it.

It began to dawn on her that she wasn't bringing much in the way of conversation either, but luckily Mark broke the silence.

"By the way, my dad did check Janice's alibi," he said, taking another large sip from his coffee.

"He did?" Julia was surprised. Dating the inspector's son was already paying off. "And?"

"She was in your pub the whole time," Mark said.

"Well, she was there, but I don't know about the whole time," Julia said. "I think she slipped out at some point."

"Apparently your waiter says she didn't leave," said Mark.

"You mean Barry?" said Julia.

Mark shrugged.

"Pfft," Julia said, reflecting on Barry's assessment of how long she had been downstairs changing the barrel. "I wouldn't trust what he's got to say. Besides, he was in and out himself, so how would he know?"

She poked angrily at her coffee with the stirrer and when she looked up again Mark had a peculiar look on his face, his eyes wide and round over his pronounced cheekbones as though he'd seen a ghost.

"What did I say?" Julia asked.

Mark tore his eyes away and brought his focus back to Julia, leaning in close to talk in a hushed voice. "Don't look now," he said. "But you remember that red-haired geezer you chased out of the Fox and Hounds? He just walked in the door."

"What?" Julia cried, spinning around so fast on her stool that it almost toppled over.

Julia's whirligig impression caught the red-haired man's attention and he wasted no time in performing one of his own, spinning quickly on his heel and charging back out of the door, shouldering aside a man in a suit who was coming the other way.

"After him!" Julia shouted, snatching up her coat and handbag from the table, but she needn't have troubled herself, Mark was already on his feet and nimbly weaving between chairs to the door.

She arrived outside on the pavement only a second after Mark, but he was standing empty-handed and scanning the high street in both directions. "He just disappeared into thin air," he said in disbelief.

Julia looked to her right and peered through the small lunchtime crowd and then to her left and clocked sight of the front of the number 10 bus.

"The bus!" she screeched pointing in its direction.

Julia took off again at a run, catching the chalkboard with her hip as she went and sending it clattering to the ground. She half turned to see the blackboard lying forlornly on the pavement. She couldn't go back for it; the chase was just too important. She let the sign lie where she had toppled it and a tingle went down her spine. She had never felt such wild abandon.

Julia charged full-pelt towards the idling bus, hearing Mark running behind her. His long strides quickly caught her up and he powered past her, shoes pounding on the pavement.

But it was to no avail. Just as he drew level with the front of the bus there was a dull hiss and the doors slowly wheeled themselves shut in his face. He threw up his hands pleadingly at the bus driver but the woman affected not to see him and smoothly pulled the vehicle out into the sparse traffic.

Julia glared an evil eye at the bus driver, which she ignored. The bus sailed past, carrying the red-haired man. Briefly, he made eye contact with her through the window, his eyes widened with surprise when he saw her and he threw himself down below the height of the glass.

Julia stood panting with her hands on her hips, watching the green single-decker trundle off down the high street. At the speed it was going, a fitter person might have considered running after it, but she knew it would gather pace once it cleared the memorial cenotaph at the corner.

"That's twice," Mark said, although Julia was in no mood to be impressed by his razor-sharp arithmetical ability. "How does he do it?"

Julia shook her head. She was still breathing heavily from the twenty odd yards that they'd run, although she tried to hide that from Mark. "He must be arriving by bus. It always waits about five minutes on Biddle High Street, so he's jumping back on board just as it goes." She had learned this to much frustration when she had briefly worked in the supermarket in King's Barrow. When she questioned the driver about it she had said it was to get the bus back on schedule. But, since Julia always ended up late for work and promptly failed her trial period, she suspected it was just so that the driver could have a crafty fag instead.

Mark's face lit up so expressively that he might as well have had a cartoon light bulb appear above it. "I'll bring the van round, we'll catch them up. I know the route well enough."

"Won't you miss work?" Julia asked.

"Stuff work," Mark said.

"Spoken like someone who has never had to deal with Jobcentre Plus," Julia said drily, but Mark was already sprinting round the corner, fishing in his pocket as he went for his keys.

Just a few moments later, he pulled around the corner in a pale-blue van and hit the brakes right by Julia. The side of the van read 'Hargreaves and Son – Painters' and was in surprisingly neat nick for a works van.

"Get in," Mark cried, gesticulating wildly.

Julia tugged at the handle but the door didn't budge.

Mark swore under his breath and reached over to open it from inside.

"The auto-locking," he explained as Julia clambered in and searched for the seat belt.

The van peeled away, and Julia looked across and saw Mark glaring intently out of the windscreen, his eyes narrow and the tip of his tongue poking rather endearingly from the corner of his mouth. He mashed the gears dramatically, obviously exhilarated with the thrill of the pursuit, but Julia couldn't help noticing that he was still sticking rigidly to the high street's twenty-mile-per-hour limit.

Julia settled back into her seat and watched the village glide sedately by outside the window. She sensed Mark relax slightly, conceding that the chase wasn't going to be quite the wild ride that he'd had in his mind's eye.

"So," Julia said. "Hargreaves and Son. What's that about?"

Mark looked over at her briefly, trying to concentrate on the traffic. "What do you mean?"

"Who is Hargreaves? And I thought your dad was a cop."

"Oh, I see. No, Hargreaves is Mum. She's the painter."

Julia felt herself cringing. Why hadn't she realized that? No reason a woman couldn't be a painter.

Mark had one of his grins on like he was about to turn the screw but then he pointed up ahead. "There it is."

Julia squinted against the sun and then caught sight of the bus, just leaving the village and merging onto the main road.

"Now I can catch them up." Mark smiled.

He pushed his foot down on the accelerator, the diesel engine responding with a deep rumble.

Then the bus indicated and pulled slowly over into a bay at the side of the road. Mark gave a deflated sigh and eased on the brakes.

"Reckon I've got time to dash out and hop on the bus?" Julia asked.

"Probably not. And I'd rather not leave you alone with that guy anyway," Mark said.

He had a good point. She was only chasing him because she thought the bloke might be a murderer. Her five foot and a tiny bit of change frame wasn't going to cut the most intimidating figure if he thought about getting rough.

The bus pulled out again and Mark brought the van up to speed behind it. "Just keep an eye on who gets off at each stop," he said to Julia. "If you see Red getting off then we can pull over."

"Right. Will do."

They followed the bus as it reached the patch of national-speed-limit road around the foot of Pagan's Hill and promptly got stuck behind a tractor. A short line of vehicles began to build up behind Mark, occasionally swerving out to the right to see if they could overtake the line of slow-moving traffic.

And in this fashion, the slowest and least adrenaline-fuelled car chase in history swept past Only Gardens and down the B-road towards King's Barrow.

When they reached the market town, traffic began to thicken up, at least compared to the sedate amounts found around Biddle Rhyne. Once or twice, Mark even had to locate the accelerator in order to stop too many other vehicles interjecting themselves between him and the bus.

As they trundled past the large supermarket on the outskirts of the town, the bus indicated left and moved off the road and into a bay.

Julia craned her head against the cold glass of the side window in order to see who was disembarking. Mark eased the van to a halt a few feet behind the bus and ignored the blare of horns as he sat idling and blocking the traffic behind him.

She kept her eyes peeled as a young family made use of the temporary traffic hold-up to cross the road, blocking her view. Her eyes lit up as the family cleared out of the way. "That's him, he's getting off!" she cried.

"Okay," Mark said, leaning his elbows on the steering wheel to get a better view of the road. "I'll find somewhere to pull in."

"What are you talking about?" Julia cried. "Just park in the lay-by."

"I can't park in there, it's a bus stop," Mark protested. The car behind him hooted again.

"For Pete's sake, Mark, this is meant to be a car chase," Julia said.

"What would my dad say?" Mark moaned, but all the same he eased the van into gear and slid into the bus stop just as the bus pulled away.

An orange Fiat sailed past, the old woman behind the wheel raising two fingers to show her appreciation of Mark's driving in no uncertain terms.

Julia paid this no heed. She hopped down from the van, and began hurrying after the redhead, who was slouching off down a footpath between two low hedges that led to the shop, apparently unaware that he was being tailed. She heard the other van door slamming and Mark's footsteps catching up behind her.

They ran side by side down the narrow pathway, bumping gently into each other in their haste, and caught up with their quarry just as he reached a covered Perspex trolley park.

Hearing them approaching, the man turned round from the line of trolleys and his face fell. His eyes darted left and right but between them Julia and Mark fully blocked the narrow mouth of the trolley park. They had him trapped.

He dipped his shoulder just slightly, his body language suggesting he was going to try and push through like he had in the Fox and Hounds, but Mark edged forward, inserting his broad frame in front of Julia, and Red seemed to think better of trying to barge past.

"Leave me alone, will you?" the man cried, looking around fruitlessly for anyone or anything that might help him. "What do you want?"

"The truth for a start," Julia said. She felt she had the moral high ground here and with Mark for back-up she felt only the slightest twinge of fear at the prospect she might be confronting a cold-blooded killer. She was intent not to let that show so she straightened up and thrust her chin in the air. "You were in the Barley Mow last Sunday."

"I wasn't, I swear," the man said, holding his hands up defensively. If he was a killer he didn't seem to have much fight in him, Julia had to admit.

"You're all over the CCTV," Julia said. Of course she knew Biddle was far too sleepy a village and Ivan was far too cheap for him ever to have put CCTV in the Barley Mow. But she was banking on Red not knowing that.

"It could have been my twin brother," the man said.

"Pull the other one," Mark replied.

The man's whole body wilted. He suddenly looked very small. "All right, fine. I was there. If anyone knows I was drinking, though, I'll be fired quicker than you can say 'Foster's Light'."

"Your job being?" Julia prompted.

"I'm a coach driver."

That made sense. He must have been the driver for the coach that brought the residents in from Abbot's Mead.

"I just figured that if I had to work on Sunday I might as well have a pint and watch the rugby. Even if it was just on my phone," he whined, the self-pity written all across his cringing body.

"More than one pint, if I recall correctly," Julia said, enjoying this moral high ground business and seeing no reason that she should abandon it now.

"Fine, fine," he conceded. "It was a couple. I won't do it again, I promise you."

Mark raised a finger to eye height and jabbed it in the man's direction. "You'd better not."

"I won't!" Then the man's eyes narrowed slightly as though something was dawning on him. "How come you two are so interested, though, anyway?"

"At the Barley Mow we take our responsibilities as publicans very seriously," Julia said and with a 'hmph' sound she turned neatly and began striding away. She turned her head and called over her shoulder as she went. "And get a better taste in beer."

Mark strode after her, quickly gaining level. "What do you think?" he asked, as they followed the footpath back towards the main road and where they'd parked the van.

"I think that with all the effort the Barley Mow puts into getting a good cask ale he should be drinking that and not the mass-produced swill."

"No, I mean, do you believe him?"

"Yeah, I do," Julia replied. "His story makes sense. There was a coachload of oldies so there had to be a driver somewhere while they were all having lunch. And if someone did tell his employers that he'd been drinking lager all afternoon before driving them back, then he'd definitely be out on his ear."

"True," Mark said. They'd reached the questionably parked painter's van now and he reached into his jeans for the keys. "I'm sorry to do this to you, but I'm well late for work now, I really need to go straight to the site."

Julia swore sharply and looked up at the clock on the top of the supermarket. She was meant to be at

Donaldson's in five minutes. The problem with having so few shifts was that she was constantly forgetting them.

"I'm supposed to be working at the shop," she said.

"Don't fret it," Mark told her. "My mum should be home. I'm sure she can give you a lift. If you don't mind meeting my parents like that."

Julia grimaced. "Fine," she said.

It wasn't how she would choose to meet her date's mother, it was true. If nothing else it was a bit early in the relationship. But maybe if she made a good impression on Mark's mum it would counterbalance the obviously terrible opinion that his dad had of her.

* * *

As Julia sat on the angled plastic seat of the bus stop, she reflected on the afternoon's revelations. So the mysterious red-headed stranger had only been guilty of a far lesser crime than running down Mrs White. He might have saved them all some trouble if he'd copped to it when they were at the meat draw rather than shoving her to the ground and legging it.

Julia tried to think who was left as a suspect with the coach driver ruled out.

Mrs Teller certainly had a motive, given Mrs White's long-standing tryst with her husband. And according to the residents in the care home, Janice had been at the Barley Mow on Sunday but then been absent for a large part of the meal. Not that Julia considered them massively reliable witnesses necessarily.

Other than Janice there was Barry, the only other person that Julia could think of who had an opportunity to swipe the major's car keys. On top of that he'd been acting shiftily ever since, he was definitely hiding something. Would being fired from the garden centre really have riled him up enough that he'd actually kill someone? Working in the Barley Mow surely wasn't that bad. Was it?

As much as she hated to admit it, she hadn't unearthed anything watertight against either of them but she was hoping that with a pinch of luck Mark might be able to persuade his dad to look more seriously into Janice and Barry's movements that day. And by extension, that should get herself out of the inspector's crosshairs.

A blue Ford hybrid glided quietly into the bay and wound its window down. "Julia, I presume?" the woman behind the wheel asked.

Julia nodded and hopped into the passenger side, dumping her handbag into the footwell. Mark's mum had shoulder-length blonde hair, with a few strands of grey showing here and there, and was wearing a warm-looking green jumper.

"Mark's been telling me about your little adventures together," Mark's mum said as she guided the car back into the traffic.

On the dash facing Julia was a little plastic toy dog with a movable head that began to jiggle as they drove. Mark's mum navigated all the way round a roundabout and pointed the car back towards Biddle Rhyne.

Julia looked out of the window and a herd of brown-haired cows with white faces watched impassively as they crawled slowly past in a queue of traffic. "Thanks ever so much for the lift, Mrs Hargreaves," she said.

Mark's mum looked over quizzically from the driver's seat, ratcheting on the handbrake as they waited at a red light. "Mrs Hargreaves?" she asked. "I'm Mrs Sandra Jones," she said, emphasizing the last name.

Julia's mouth formed itself into a tight line and she felt herself flushing with embarrassment. She scrambled desperately for something to say.

"I'm going to guess you're not a painter either," she managed eventually.

The other woman looked blank for a moment and then broke out into a grin, instantly showing a strong resemblance to her son despite their very different faces. "I think Mark's been pulling your leg, darling," she said.

Julia sighed and watched the fields begin to glide past again. "Yes, he does that."

"Whereabouts am I heading for?" the very definitely Mrs Jones asked her.

"Do you know Donaldson's, just off Biddle High Street?" Julia asked.

"I do."

"Right there, please. I'm already late," Julia said wretchedly.

"I would step on it for you, but if I got caught speeding my husband would never let me hear the end of it," Mrs Jones replied.

"That's okay. I've only myself to blame."

"You got distracted trying to solve a murder?" Mrs Jones asked.

Despite what she'd said, Julia could see the car's speedometer hovering slightly above 60. The dog on the dashboard nodded its approval.

"Something like that," Julia muttered.

* * *

Julia thanked Mark's mum one more time as she sprang out of the car door, hurling it shut behind her. According to the clock on the car's dash she was about twenty minutes late. Actually, by her standards that was practically early. She scooted through into the shop, squeezing past Mr Pegg coming out in the other direction, the off-key bell chiming overhead as she entered.

Donaldson stood at the till, tufts of strawberry-red hair shooting off in all directions. His eyes bulged and the veins criss-crossing his pale face stood out. He was not in a good mood.

"Sorry, sorry, Mr Donaldson," Julia sang as she started towards the counter, pulling her crumpled work shirt from where it lay crushed into a ball at the bottom of her bag.

Rather than lift the counter for her to pass like she had expected, Donaldson stood impassively with his arms folded across his chest. Julia looked up at him pleadingly.

"No, I'm sorry, Julia," he said, not looking sorry at all. "But enough is enough."

Julia became acutely aware of a pair of customers browsing the magazine rack behind her. She seriously didn't want to grovel, but she needed this job. Sally was a saint for covering most of her outgoings as it was.

"I got stuck in King's Barrow. There was this bus and…" Julia trailed off under her boss's steely gaze. "It won't happen again, I promise."

"It's not just being late," Mr Donaldson growled in reply. "Although goodness knows I've put up with plenty of that from you. But I've had complaints. Being rude and stand-offish to customers. And Mr Smedley told me he came here the other day and found it closed at five to six. Running off early? That's wage theft, Miss Ford. You should count yourself lucky I'm not on the phone to the police."

Julia's eyes dropped to the floor. "I had a good reason," she said quietly, although she knew that she didn't, not as far as Donaldson would be concerned. This stupid investigation of hers had gone too far already and she was still no closer to finding out who had killed Mrs White. Or convincing the inspector that she hadn't done it herself.

Donaldson unfolded his arms to reach over the countertop and snatch the work shirt from Julia's hand. "Now go on, get out of here," he instructed.

With her cheeks burning and her eyes still on the floor she turned and fled past the loitering customers and back out onto the street.

A cold wind came in off the moors carrying with it the promise of rain and tugging at loose strands of her hair. She sniffed, telling herself it was the chill air but at the same time fighting back that compelling urge to cry. Not here, she resolved, not on the street with everyone around. She could at least make it back to the privacy of her home.

Chapter 14

Rain came down hard outside. Julia watched from the kitchen window with a saucer in one hand and the steaming, broad-rimmed mug of tea in the other, enjoying the feeling of the warmth coming up through her fingertips. Simple home comforts. They had helped to soften the blow a little bit. At least she'd stopped crying now.

Rainy weather was always good reading weather as far as Julia was concerned, but her copy of *Rebecca* lay abandoned in the living room; the ferociousness of the pelting raindrops was so mesmerizing that she couldn't tear herself away. In the distance, a dull peal of thunder was just distinguishable over the muffled sound of the rain.

The small square of patio outside the kitchen window was an inch underwater now, and rising. The weeds that choked the paving slabs had first started to gently float as the water lifted them but now were lost from view underneath the surface. The lawn beyond was presumably just as waterlogged, but the length of the grass hid the effect from sight for the time being.

Julia's phone chirped, rousing her from her semi-hypnosis. She grabbed it off the kitchen counter to see Sally's smiling features beneath the 'accept call' button.

"Hi, Julia," Sally said when she answered. "Ivan's having a small crisis here at the pub and he wants every pair of hands he can get."

"What's the matter?" Julia asked, although looking from the corner of her eye at the state of the garden she thought she could guess.

"The cellar's starting to flood," Sally said, confirming Julia's suspicions. "Ivan says he'll give time and a half if you can come in and help move some of the perishables up out of harm's way. Don't worry, most of it's not that heavy."

"Sure," Julia said, thinking that she wasn't really in a position to turn down any work. Anyway, it would be good to get her mind off Donaldson's.

"Thanks, chicken," Sally said. "I'll be over to pick you up in about five minutes."

Julia hung up the phone and then went searching underneath the stairs for her wellie boots and her waterproof jacket. Rumpkin came over from the living room to investigate what was going on.

Julia looked down at the dog. He looked back at her and licked his own nose. He had a way of cheering her up when she was down. "I suppose you can come, too, if you promise not to get in the way," Julia said.

Rumpkin woofed in reply.

* * *

Sally drove slowly. Even so, great curtains of water rose up from either side of the car as it made its way back down the lane towards the Barley Mow. A very small, petty part of Julia hoped that they would pass one of the cyclists who she so often got stuck behind when driving down here, but, unsurprisingly given the deluge, the whole stretch of road was deserted.

The fields were awash with water: a cold grey sheen stretching away underneath the long grass. The river must have burst its banks already and the water level was up at the height of the rhynes. Looking out over this marshy aspect, it was easy to remember that this was all reclaimed land. Right now it seemed the sea was doing its best to claim it back.

In the middle distance, herds of brown cows, their white faces slick with water, waded despondently through their pastures while high overhead, black storm clouds floated with a deceptive gentleness over the landscape.

Sally parked the car up directly outside the front door of the pub, minimizing the distance they'd have to dash through the rain, and looked over at her passenger. "Ready?" she asked.

Julia nodded. "Ready."

They both grabbed their door handles and hopped down onto the gravel with a splash. Sally instantly took off towards the shelter of the pub, pulling her hood up even for the few yards she had to go.

Julia rushed around and opened the boot of the car, but rather than springing into action as he usually did, Rumpkin sat stubbornly looking at Julia while the freezing raindrops drummed down on the hood of her waterproof.

"Come on, you useless mutt," Julia implored him, but he just backed himself further into the car.

There was another peal of thunder, closer this time, and Rumpkin bedded himself down, hiding his face in his paws, and began to quiver.

Julia gave an exasperated sigh and wiped the water from her eyes. She reached in and grabbed the terrier with both hands, although he gave only a token resistance to being picked up, squirming pathetically in his mistress's hands.

She managed to get the boot of the car closed with one elbow and then, with Rumpkin cradled to her chest, she hurried over the gravel and into the parlour, unceremoniously depositing her dog onto the flagstones as she crossed the threshold. Rumpkin shook energetically and Julia flinched away from the spray of droplets he sent arcing in all directions.

She glared and was about to remonstrate with him when she realized that she was already so wet that a few more drops really made no difference. Then, all fear of the storm and the rain apparently already forgotten, Rumpkin loped across the room with his tail held high and planted himself down in front of the crimson embers of the log fire.

Julia was just unzipping her dripping-wet jacket when Ivan appeared from the staff doorway, straining under the weight of a large cardboard box of bar snacks. He placed them on top of the existing stack of them by the till.

"Julia, glad you could join us," he greeted her, red-faced and panting, placing his hands on top of his pile of boxes. He looked down at her footwear. "I'm glad you've got your wellies on, you're going to need them. Get yourself down into the cellar; Sally can show you what needs moving."

Julia glanced down and saw that Ivan's own polished black work shoes were sodden through, along with the hems of his trousers.

Julia hung her coat up and gave a jealous look over her shoulder at Rumpkin who was already snoring in front of the fire and well on his way to drying out. She headed through the gap in the bar, squeezed past the stacked boxes and then through the doorway to the series of corridors which formed the heart of the pub.

She was just making her way down the dimly lit passageway towards the cellar when she came to a sudden halt. She thought she saw the outline of a person in the nook next to the spare cutlery cupboard. She squinted into the gloom. There was definitely someone there, dressed all in black and apparently doing their best not to be seen, pressing themselves into the recess in the wall.

Julia took a cautious step forwards, taking some comfort in the fact that Ivan should still be within earshot. "Hello?" she asked.

The shadow figure grunted, and Barry stepped forward into the light of the corridor, such as it was, shoving his phone hastily into his pocket as he did so. He smoothed down some of the creases in his black work shirt.

"I was just seeing if there was anything here that needed moving," he mumbled, and headed off in the direction of the kitchens, where Julia was fairly certain nothing was in any risk of flooding whatsoever.

She placed her hand on her heart while it stopped beating so quickly.

Ivan stuck his head round the doorway from the parlour. "Come on, Julia, I'm not paying you just to stand around, you know."

Julia muttered an apology to Ivan and headed through the archway that led to the cellar staircase, taking the uneven stone steps carefully.

The cellar of the pub was large, running underneath most of the footprint of the building. The uneven floor sloped away from the staircase, going deeper underground as it went along. Nearby, just next to where Julia now stood, were rows of metal casks that attached to the pumps upstairs by a byzantine network of tubes that only made sense to Ivan.

Further down the room were stacks of cardboard boxes containing bar snacks and assorted receipts and other paperwork for the pub. Normally these stacks would have stretched all the way to the far wall, but already the rising water had reached the lowest points of the cellar floor, the chill dark water rippling ever so slightly in the light of the dim, bare bulbs suspended from the ceiling.

Sally was busy pushing a box of manilla folders up the gentle slope of the floor away from the water. Evidently she'd been hard at work before going to fetch Julia because several stacks of boxes had been shifted from their usual home up to higher ground near the beer barrels.

Sally paused from her work, her face flushed from her latest efforts.

"Can you take some of these upstairs? I'm going to run out of space to push them to otherwise," she huffed.

Julia nodded and grabbed the first box of the nearest pile. It wasn't too heavy but as she staggered up the cellar stairs with it, she could tell she was going to be feeling a serious burn in her leg muscles before the day was out.

She teetered carefully along the corridors, her view partially obscured by the files sticking up from the box, and she cursed mentally at Ivan for his haphazard filing system. The odds were that most of this stuff was probably out of date and not worth the effort of keeping. Still, at least he was paying her well to preserve it.

She had made it all the way back to the parlour before her inevitable fall. The uneven flagstones behind the bar caught the toe of her boot and she pitched forward, the folders tumbling from the box and going sliding in all directions across the floor.

Julia let out a little cry as she landed, more out of surprise than any real hurt. Rumpkin let out a low woof and came over to investigate, dripping onto several of the folders as he did so.

"Oh, go away, you're not helping," Julia said, shoving the animal's nose out of her face as she struggled up onto her knees and did her best to gather the folders up and get them back into the box.

When she had the last folder in, Julia heaved the box up and placed it on top of the bar, well out of Rumpkin's reach.

She was just about to head back down to the cellar for the next box when something on the floor caught her eye: a small white rectangle of paper that must have escaped from the files when she dropped them.

Julia scooped the errant piece of paper up and was about to deposit it back in the box when she noticed the writing on the front. The sheet of paper was folded up like a letter, with Barry's name written in a gentle looping handwriting. It was a woman's, Julia was sure of it.

Unlike the aged, yellow paperwork making up the rest of the files, this was crisp and white. Undoubtedly it had been shoved hastily into the recesses of the filing to keep it hidden. *But why?*

She turned the paper over in her fingers. It was neatly folded up and she stood agonizing over whether to open it, torn between her better conscience at reading someone else's correspondence and the burning desire to know if it had something to do with Barry's strange disappearances and Mrs White's death.

She had just made up her mind to read the letter when the outside door came flying open, hitting the wall with a bang.

The major stood framed in the doorway, rain gusting in around him. "Gosh, it's filthy weather out there," he observed astutely.

"Major, what are you doing here? We're closed," Julia said.

"Ah, piffle, I need a drink. Especially after that soaking," the major said, pulling his flat cap from his head and holding it outside in order to wring the water from it.

Just then there was a terrific, echoing boom of thunder that seemed to make the whole building tremble. Rumpkin gave a terrified yelp and went flying as fast as he could across the flagstones, through the major's legs and out into the storm.

"Rumpkin!" Julia cried, hastily dropping the note back on top of the box and running over to the doorway. The major edged aside as she arrived.

She stood in the doorway, scanning the car park, but the rain was driving down so ferociously that she was hardly able to see more than twenty feet in front of her.

Already Rumpkin was out of sight, with no sign of which direction he'd taken. She called his name again to no answer.

"Ah, that is a ruddy shame," the major said, also peering out into the storm. "Here doggy, doggy."

Julia looked at the rain hammering down on the gravel with such force that it was bouncing back up a centimetre from the ground. With weather like this, if she didn't get Rumpkin back soon he was liable to freeze. That wasn't even considering that most of his favourite hidey-holes were probably underwater by now, or that the visibility was so low drivers would have no chance of spotting him.

"I'm going after him," Julia declared, grabbing her still-dripping waterproof from the peg.

"You'll get wet," the major told her.

"Tell Sally where I've gone," Julia said, stepping out into the deluge.

The major's reply was just audible as she stepped out into the hiss of the rain. "I thought *you* were Sally."

Julia hauled the door shut, fighting against the wind to do so. She stomped through the puddles of the car park calling Rumpkin's name as she went. The pub's sign swung violently overhead, the spotlights at the top of it winking in and out.

By the time she had reached the looping chains that separated the car park from the road she was already soaked through and her face was raw from the freezing rain. She looked both ways up the lane but she couldn't even see as far as the bend in the road. It was hopeless.

Julia could already feel tears beginning to join the rain rushing down her cheeks. She picked a direction without much real thought to it and ploughed on down the lane, crossing a concrete bridge over the swollen rhyne and clambering over the five-bar gate into the swamp of a field beyond it, following one of Rumpkin's favourite walking routes.

* * *

Julia staggered back into the parlour of the Barley Mow an hour later dazed, dripping and still empty-handed. The rain had slackened to a light drizzle now and the sun shone weakly through gaps in the clouds, but that had done nothing to lift her spirits.

As she wrestled the door shut behind her, Sally leapt from her stool at the bar and hurried over.

"Oh, goodness, chicken, what were you thinking? You're soaked through." Sally cooed over her friend, helping her peel off her sodden waterproof.

"Rumpkin got scared by the thunder and ran away," Julia managed between sniffs.

"I know, the major told me. But never mind that; Rumpkin can take care of himself."

"We both know that dog's an idiot," Julia said.

Sally didn't reply but guided Julia gently towards the fireplace where the logs were crackling away fiercely, the flames leaping and dancing as they spread their warmth about the parlour. As she lowered herself into the low-backed wooden chair, Julia became aware of an array of worried faces about her.

Sally, of course, fussing over her and fetching her own relatively dry coat to use as a blanket. The major in the seat opposite was awake for once and offered some muttered condolences about Rumpkin. A half-drunk pint of bitter sat on the table in front of him – evidently he'd talked someone into serving him. Julia supposed it would have been harsh to turn the old man away in the middle of the storm.

Ivan emerged from behind the bar, a large glass of red wine clutched in one of his equally red hands. "It's on the house," he said softly, placing it down on the table in front of Julia. "Maybe it will warm you up a bit, eh?"

Julia fished out a tissue to wipe her nose and did her best to give Ivan a smile.

As Ivan took a seat next to her, Julia looked up at the empty bar. Barry was notable by his absence. Her mind flitted briefly back to the note she'd found among the paperwork she'd hauled up from the cellar. She could see from across the room that it had gone. Most likely Barry had taken it. She drew her knees up and hugged them to her chest. So much for that lead, some sleuth that she was turning out to be.

Behind the bar the boxes were stacked up to above head height. Above Julia's head height, at any rate.

"You saved everything downstairs from the water, then?" Julia asked.

"Yes, all safe and dry," Ivan said.

"Sorry I wasn't much help."

"Oh, don't worry about that. Let's just hope your dog is all right. You'll probably find him waiting for you when you get home," said Ivan.

"Probably," Julia sighed, although she didn't believe it.

She could just feel another wave of tears fighting their way to the surface when she heard a loud series of barks from the direction of the bar and sat bolt upright. It was unmistakably her Rumpkin.

The door to the staff area behind the bar opened and Rumpkin came charging through. He was soaked to his skin, and water flew from his coat all over the bar as he ran over the flagstones. His soggy paws fought for purchase and lost and he came tumbling and rolling to a halt at Julia's feet. With an excited bark he scrambled upright and then sprung into her lap where she enveloped him in a huge hug. He was shivering with cold but she hugged him close and edged the chair as close to the fire as she dared.

"Oh, goodness, boy. Where have you come from?" Julia asked, but Rumpkin's only answer was to cover her face in affectionate licks.

Julia managed to crane her neck enough that she was free of the excited dog's tongue and looked over towards the bar. Standing in the arch of the doorway was Barry, one hand resting on the doorframe. There was just a hint of a smile on his ever-sullen features.

"Barry! Thank you so much. Where did you find him?" Julia gushed.

Barry gave a big shrug of his shoulders. "Just around," he said.

"What do you mean 'around'?" Sally asked, her eyes narrowing. "Where was he?"

Barry gave a little twitch of his head to indicate that he didn't know. "He was just around the back of the pub, I heard him scratching at the back door," he said.

Julia did her best to suppress Rumpkin's latest attack of adoration and studied Barry. He had removed his coat, but he'd obviously been outside because his trousers were soaked to the thighs and his shoes were glistening with water. She opened her mouth to question him but thought better of it. Wherever he'd been, he obviously wasn't about to tell them. As much as he was behaving shiftily, right now Julia couldn't summon up the energy to care very much.

Where he had sloped off to, what he'd done with the note; he could keep those secrets. For now at least. Right this moment, Julia was just pleased to have little Rumpkin returned to her.

She exchanged a meaningful glance with Sally and her friend sat back into her seat, arms folded and her lips pressed tight together.

Chapter 15

Julia had spent most of the next day underneath a blanket in her pyjamas and the rest of it dressed but underneath a blanket. But crucially she had spent it underneath a blanket with Rumpkin who seemed equally keen for some cuddle time after his misadventures the day before.

Gradually, Julia's mood lifted but reached a fairly low plateau as she couldn't escape the fact that she was now completely unemployed and still no closer to clearing her name with DI Jones.

Then, in mid-afternoon when she was just debating whether it was worth shifting from underneath the blanket in order to make a pot of tea, she received a text message that managed to put her into a good mood.

'Dinner, tonight? On me,' Mark asked.

Julia's tiny squeal of excitement stirred Rumpkin from his slumber and he looked questioningly up at his mistress.

"You're not coming to this one," she told him in no uncertain terms.

* * *

The waiter gently deposited the plates on the table with a warm smile and disappeared again.

Julia looked down at the shellfish lining her plate and wondered how on Earth she was meant to eat the things. This was a proper date, for pity's sake. Her first one in a very long while. She sighed, she should have played it safe and ordered the gnocchi. It would probably be bland but at least she wouldn't have to work out how to shell it.

"Something wrong?" Mark asked.

He was wearing a very similar outfit to what he'd worn in the Stag and Hounds the other night – well-cut jeans and a plain but flattering T-shirt – somehow managing to look like he had just thrown it on but also look at home in the upmarket surrounding of the restaurant. For her part, Julia had struggled into her little black dress and although it had filled her with confidence when riding in the taxi she was feeling self-conscious and overdressed now.

She flashed a smile, lifted her fork up and did her best to make headway into one of the shells, praying silently that she wouldn't send the crustacean firing off her plate. "No, nothing's wrong."

Mark was tucking heartily into the lamb chops he'd ordered. He certainly had an appetite but at least he had the table manners not to talk with his mouth full. He was already ahead of most of the men Julia had dated.

He swallowed a mouthful of lamb. "I thought you might appreciate it if we made a rule and said no talk about murder at the dinner table. Perhaps, if we're feeling bold, we could avoid the topic of crime altogether?"

Julia raised her glass of white wine. "Sounds perfect."

She took a drink and then the two of them sat in silence for some time, working away at their meals. Eventually Julia managed to prise one of the shellfish open and actually taste a mouthful of it. It was nice, although it might have been nicer when it was warmer.

"How's the food?" Mark asked.

"Good," she replied, "good."

She couldn't help but notice that Mark's plate was almost half-empty, and his wine completely gone.

"Shall I top you up?" She offered the bottle towards him but he held his hand over his glass.

"Better not, I'm driving," he replied.

Of course, that was the downside of going to the glitz and bright lights of King's Barrow: you had to get there somehow.

"You should have said before we ordered a bottle," Julia said.

Mark swallowed the final mouthful of his food and shrugged. "It barely costs more for the bottle than two glasses and this way you can have as much as you want."

Julia's eyes narrowed. "Are you trying to get me drunk, Mark?"

He laughed. "No, it's just a happy by-product."

Julia took the bottle and topped herself up. "The benefits of taking a taxi, I suppose."

"I can give you a lift home, if you like. Save you a taxi fare."

That's forward, Julia thought. There's no way he's coming back to my place tonight.

* * *

Julia stood facing the front door, digging through her handbag for the keys. She could feel Mark standing close behind her, his breath warm on the back of her neck. Her heart fluttered. She hadn't been in this situation for quite some time.

When she got the door open it was dark downstairs. That avoided some awkwardness: it meant that Sally had already retired upstairs. Hopefully she wouldn't be popping down to say hello.

Someone else was there, though, as there was an excited snuffling sound and Rumpkin skittered over from the living room, wagging his tail excitedly to see his mistress home. She allowed him to lick her fingers a couple of times and then he bounded behind her to give Mark a good sniff.

"Can I make you coffee?" Julia asked.

Mark nodded. "That would be nice."

Julia made a sweeping gesture towards the living room. "Make yourself comfortable."

As Mark made his way over towards the sofa, Julia headed into the kitchen and flicked the kettle on.

Equal parts tipsy and excited, she found her hands shaking as she measured the grinds out into the cafetière. "Oh, get a hold of yourself, woman," she admonished herself.

She poked around in the top cupboards to find the nice cups with matching saucers and blew the dust off them before placing them carefully onto the tray. The kettle seemed to be taking an age and a half to boil, and after waiting impatiently she gave up on it and went on through to the living room to see how her guest was doing.

Mark was standing in the centre of the room with just the standard lamp on in the corner, casting a long shadow across the carpet.

There was a shocked, almost ill expression on his face.

Julia gasped. "What's the matter?"

Very slowly, as though it pained him to move, he held up his hands and showed her the curious object that he was holding.

She didn't recognize it at first. A gardening magazine, not that she'd ever bought one. For a moment she thought that Mark might have had it with him, stuffed away inside his coat pocket.

But then, as her eyes adjusted to the dim light, she realized that a score of letters had been cut out of it leaving behind a pattern of neat squares.

"I've never seen that before," Julia said, her words coming out in a hoarse whisper. Her mouth suddenly felt dry and heavy.

Mark was looking down at the removed letters in horror. "It's the magazine that the death threat was made from, isn't it?" he said.

Julia swallowed. "Yes." Even if she had never seen it before, she knew that much was true.

Mark looked up and met her eye. He was staring at her now and she felt herself wilting under his gaze.

"Did you find it in here? I have no idea how it got here. I swear." She could feel the hot rush of tears welling up in her eyes. *How could this have happened?*

"I… I…" Mark stammered, lost for words. He looked rapidly from the terrible magazine to Julia and back. "I have to go."

He let the magazine fall from his hands as though he was suddenly afraid to be holding it and with that he brushed past Julia and rushed towards the door, his coat forgotten and discarded over the back of the sofa.

Julia held a hand out pleadingly after him. "Don't go! I've never seen it before. I don't know how it got here. You won't tell your dad, will you?"

He didn't turn around, but kept going until he was outside. He shouted back over his shoulder. "I have to," he said and pushed the front door shut behind him with a slam that made the whole house rattle.

Julia sank down onto her knees and sobbed, deep, ugly gasps that shook her whole body.

Rumpkin began barking and running laps of the living room, manic with surprise and directionless excitement as he tried to work out what the game was.

Upstairs, there was the sound of feet pounding across the floorboards, but Julia barely registered them. Sally came crashing down the stairs so fast that she slipped on the bottom step and went staggering into the wall, fighting for balance. Her mouth swung open as she took in the scene before her.

"What happened?" Sally demanded, her eyes ablaze. "Did he hurt you? That swine, wait till I get my hands on him." She held a clenched fist up before her, trembling with rage.

"It's not that," Julia managed between sobs. She held up a finger and pointed. "Look."

Sally gave her a puzzled look and stalked past to where she was pointing. Rumpkin chose this moment to bounce past and clipped her shin, sending her crashing to the ground. "Stupid, dog," she muttered.

Sally regained her feet and then stooped to pick up the magazine, examining the cover.

"*Gardening Weekly*? I hate gardening as much as you, but is it really that big a deal? How much did you drink tonight, chicken?"

"Look inside," Julia said weakly. Her sobs had subsided now to a sniffle and, all thoughts of dignity gone, she wiped her nose with the back of her hand. She was a streaked mess of mascara by this point anyway, nothing she did was going to matter.

Sally duly flipped the cover open. "Some letters have been snipped out," she said. And then it began to dawn on her. "This is the magazine that was used for the death threat sent to Mrs White."

Julia sniffed again and nodded. She threw herself down into the armchair.

"Mark had this on him? So *he* wrote the note?" Sally asked.

Julia dabbed at her eyes with the corner of the blanket. "No, he found it here."

Sally looked unconvinced. "Here in the living room? Are you sure?"

"Yes. He was so shocked when he found it here, I'm certain of it."

"But I've been in all day," Sally replied. "No one else has been here, just me and Rumpkin. I would have noticed if someone had broken in."

"I don't know how it got here then," Julia said.

The two women's eyes met across the room.

"You don't think I…" Sally trailed off.

"No, of course I don't, Sally," Julia said.

Sally placed the magazine down onto the side table. "We'd better leave that for the police to look at," she said.

"They're probably already on their way here to arrest me," Julia said and the tears began to flow again.

Sally rushed across the room and enveloped her in a warm hug and made delicate shushing noises at her. Julia clutched at her back, drawing her in closer and burying the mess that was her face into Sally's curls.

Rumpkin decided to join in as well and tried to nuzzle his way into the middle of the two women, but sensing that he wasn't the centre of attention he soon lost interest and trundled away.

Sally eased herself away and glanced around. "Rumpkin! No!" she shouted.

The overexcited animal had made his way to the side table and was enthusiastically licking at the magazine.

"Get off there," Sally said, pushing Rumpkin away with one hand and snatching up the soiled magazine with the other. She held it up to examine it. "It's covered in dog slobber." She scrunched up her nose in distaste.

"That's not all it's covered in," Julia said. Gingerly, she reached forward and took the magazine between thumb and forefinger and peered closely at the cover. "It's smeared with chocolate spread."

"What?" Sally leaned in closer to get a better look. "You're right. There are little lines of it all over. Whatever can that be about?"

Julia collapsed back into the chair. "That cow," she said.

"What?"

"Janice Teller. Or whoever it was who made the note. They spread chocolate on the magazine and they posted it through our letter box. And then of course Rumpkin grabbed it and brought it in."

"Someone planted it here? Via Rumpkin? Why?"

"Probably because I've been putting my big nose in snooping around. Now it's going to look like I wrote the note isn't it? That pretty much seals it. No one's ever going to believe me now."

"We could just get rid of it," Sally said. "We could put it in the gas fire right now. Who would know?"

"But Mark's seen it. His dad's going to believe him even if the magazine's gone. And as far as the inspector thinks, I keep dangling it in front of his nose and then hiding it like I'm toying with him."

Sally flopped down next to the chair and put her head on Julia's knee. "What are you going to do?" she whispered.

"I'm going to sit here and wait for Mark's dad to come and arrest me."

The wait felt like an interminably long time. The two women sat in silence with only the sound of Rumpkin's laboured snoring filling the room until there was a sharp knock at the door and Sally rose to answer it.

In the end it wasn't Mark's dad who came to arrest her, but a young, uniformed pair of constables with stern faces. They didn't ask many questions. One of them put the handcuffs on Julia while reading her her rights and the other picked up the magazine and sealed it meticulously into a clear, labelled bag.

The world seemed to spin around her as Julia walked towards the marked police car parked across the end of the drive. As the car pulled off and made its way down the street she could feel the curtain of every bedroom window they passed twitch open.

Chapter 16

Mr Hart was the duty solicitor at King's Barrow Police Station that night. He sat with Julia in the painfully functional interrogation room.

The solicitor hadn't filled her with confidence. For a start, the cheap, ill-fitting suit he wore spoke volumes about his professional quality and his attention to detail. And when she had gone over her version of events with him she could sense an undercurrent of disbelief.

"And you're sure that you want to maintain that you're not guilty?" he had asked at the end of it.

Now they sat next to each other on the cold metal chairs in silence. The room was whitewashed and windowless. The only furniture were the folding chairs and the table in the middle with a solid metal fixture for attaching handcuffs to. Thank God for small mercies, at least the police hadn't deemed it necessary to use that.

Julia looked around, not that there was anything to look at. She'd expected a two-way mirror to be on one wall so she could glare confrontationally at it, but there wasn't even that. Instead, there was a minuscule camera secreted in one corner which didn't really have the same effect.

After what seemed like an unreasonably long time, the door behind her opened and DI Jones slouched in, his heavy build crossing the room slowly to the other side of the table where he lowered himself into one of the chairs. Julia was sure that she heard the strain of metal akin to the sound effects used on *Titanic* or *The Poseidon Adventure*.

He sat looking across the table, making a deep rattling wheezing sound through his nose.

Eventually Julia broke the silence. "Shouldn't there be two of you?"

The inspector left a long pause before answering. "Two of us? Why?"

"I thought you played good cop, bad cop," Julia said.

Jones grunted. "You've seen too much TV. It's just me."

Julia scowled. He'd said that to her before and it only went to highlight how incompetent the man's deductive reasoning skills were. *Just one bad-at-his-job cop, then.*

"Shall we move on?" Hart suggested.

Jones shrugged. "Fine." He flipped a file open onto the table and produced the incriminating magazine from it, holding it up in its clear evidence bag for Julia to see. "Do you know what this is?"

"It's a gardening magazine," Julia replied tersely.

"It is indeed."

Julia folded her arms across her chest. She wished that she'd had the foresight to change out of her little black dress before the police had arrived for her. On top of the mess of her mascara she now had goose pimples all over her exposed skin. Anyone seeing her in the station would surely think she was in for soliciting. "Well, it's not mine," she replied, "I've no interest in gardening, why Would I buy a gardening magazine?"

"To make a death threat," Jones said bluntly.

Julia had known it was coming but she still flinched when he laid the charge before her.

"We know from the manager at the garden centre that Mrs White received just such a note," he continued. "It's also exactly the sort of magazine that would be lying about in Mrs White's office. I've been told that you broke in there on one occasion following a disagreement about your dog" – he made a point of looking down at his notes – "your dog, Rumpkin."

If she ever got her hands on Mark she was going to throttle him. He must have told his dad. Well, she was glad that he scuttled out of the house before they got any further than making coffee.

Against her will, Julia could feel herself pouting at the injustice of it. It should be Mrs White in here being grilled. If only someone hadn't run her down.

"She dognapped him," Julia said.

"And this made you angry?" Jones suggested.

Despite all her fury, Julia could tell she was on thin ice here. She chose her next words carefully. "A little. But I lifted the sash window to her office to let him free and that was that."

"You didn't feel the need to get even, then?" asked Jones.

"Certainly not." Julia lifted her chin into the air. "I was just happy to have little Rumpkin back."

"I see," Jones replied stonily. "And how do you think this magazine came to be in your house, if you claim not to have bought it?"

Julia sat up straight in her chair. "Well, Rumpkin brought it in."

Even Jones's previously immobile façade crumbled slightly at this. "You're saying that your dog bought it?"

"Not bought it, brought it, you great oaf."

Hart laid a steadying hand on her forearm.

"The dog brought it in?" Jones corrected himself.

"Yes," Julia said. "The magazine is smeared with chocolate spread. Someone dangled it through the letter box knowing that he'd take the thing inside and lick the chocolate off it. It was planted."

Jones brought a pen out, gave it a click while maintaining eye contact across the table, and then began to scribble something in his notebook. "I've not heard that one before," he said quietly to himself.

He had a few more questions for her, mostly around where she was at particular times and who might have seen her. And then without any comment, he lifted his great bulk from the chair and drifted out of the room.

Julia contorted herself in her chair just in time to see the heavy metal door swing shut behind him with a clang. "Where's he gone?" she asked.

Hart was shuffling his own papers together on the table. "Gone to see if he can hold you overnight, I imagine," he said. He didn't sound too bothered either way.

"Well, I have other clients to attend to," the solicitor said, rising. "The inspector should be back shortly."

"Wait? That's it?" Julia asked.

The man gave a shrug, causing his suit jacket to slip slightly at the shoulders, and rapped on the door to be let out.

As it turned out, he was wrong about the inspector being back 'shortly'. It was over an hour before Jones returned, leaving Julia to shift uncomfortably on the metal seat as she considered her fate. By the time he came back she was bursting for a pee but she did her best to appear cool and composed.

After his habitual pause to sit and wheeze in her direction, Jones plonked a beige plastic ring onto the table. "Do you know what this is, Miss Ford?"

She craned forward to look at the thing. "For playing quoits?" she suggested.

"A sterling guess, but no. It's an ankle tag."

"An ankle tag?"

"Yes, you've made bail," Jones replied. He didn't look too happy about it.

"You don't look very happy about it," Julia said.

Jones scowled. "I don't like seeing criminals out on the streets."

"I'm not a criminal," Julia said.

Jones hefted the ankle tracker. "Well, if the tag fits."

Julia stared despondently at the device on the table.

"This is the new model," Jones said, giving the ankle tag a pat. "It's got all the bells and whistles."

"Lucky me," Julia said.

"Yes, indeed. Lucky you. Your curfew has been set at 8 p.m., so you need to be home by then every day. If you're not, then this is going to let me know."

The talk went on for a little longer as the inspector told Julia how to charge the tag and then he clipped it around her bare ankle.

She looked down at it gloomily, wishing she at least had trousers to cover it. "Am I free to go?" she asked quietly.

"You are." Jones leaned in close to her. She could practically feel the bristles of his moustache on her cheek. "But just remember, when you slip up – and you will slip up – I'm going to be there."

Julia shuddered.

Jones stood and pulled the door open. Julia took this as her cue to leave and, with her head down, she went hurrying out of the door.

Chapter 17

When Julia finally made it back out into the reception area of the police station she found Sally waiting for her. Sally's eyes were bloodshot with deep, dark bags under them and she generally looked like she hadn't slept. In fact, she looked like utter crap. Julia could only imagine the state that she must look.

As soon as Sally saw her she sprinted over and folded her up into a warm hug. "God I'm so glad they've let you out, I've been so worried about you."

Julia buried her head into her friend's shoulder and did her best to hold back her tears. "Thank you so much for bailing me out," she said, her head muffled in the material of Sally's coat.

"Don't be silly, of course I would."

"How did you afford it?" Sally had been generous during Julia's stint of underemployment, but Julia knew her friend's pockets didn't run that deep.

"Oh, never mind that," Sally said. She prised herself away from Julia and took a step back. "You must be freezing," she said. She unbuttoned her coat and bundled Julia into it like a toddler.

"Now you'll be cold," Julia protested weakly, looking at Sally's bare arms and midriff that her T-shirt left exposed.

"Don't be daft, chicken," Sally said. She linked her arm into Julia's. "Come on, let's get you back home."

Julia allowed herself to be led out of the door and down the arch of concrete steps to the pavement. She was beginning to warm up now she had a coat on, but she was still painfully conscious that the ankle tag was on full display; she could feel the eyes of every passer-by glancing down at it and passing silent judgement. Despite the warmth of the snug coat, she shivered.

"Where's the car?" Julia asked, when she couldn't spot it in any of the parking bays at the front of the station. She hoped Sally hadn't parked too far away, she couldn't bear to parade around with this tag much longer.

"I took the bus in." Even as she said it, Sally guided Julia to the Perspex wall of a bus shelter and sat down against the flimsy plastic bench. A man in a dark grey suit shuffled along it to make room for them.

"Oh," Julia said. She ached to be home, the last thing she wanted was to wait for a stupid bus.

The bus seemed to take hours to arrive, the morning traffic growing busier as they waited. Every curious look down at her ankle made her want to curl up and just die. When it did finally arrive, she made straight for the back seats and threw herself down. At least cocooned here between the seats in someone else's coat she could shield herself from the world, but she was inwardly furious with Sally for not bringing the car. The ride home passed in morose silence as she watched the bare, autumn fields pass by and tried not to think about the hole she'd found herself in.

It wasn't until they reached home and there was no car on the driveway that it finally clicked.

"You sold the car, didn't you?" Julia gasped.

Sally didn't reply, just unlocked the front door and stepped in, rubbing her arms to warm them up a bit.

There was a noisy yip from the living room and Rumpkin came bounding in, leaping into the air with excitement and almost knocking Julia from her feet when they collided.

"Oh, Rumpkin," she said, rubbing him behind both ears as he licked as much of her as he could get hold of. "If only you knew the trouble you've caused."

* * *

Julia bathed, washed and combed her hair and then wrapped herself up in her dressing gown despite the fact it was almost midday.

When she arrived downstairs, she found both a tea and a coffee waiting for her on the side table, each of them steaming away.

"I wasn't sure which you'd feel like," Sally explained.

Julia did her best to look grateful and picked up the tea as she settled down into the chair, cradling it in her hands and enjoying the heat.

"We need to find whoever killed Mrs White," Sally said matter-of-factly. "That idiot of a police officer isn't going to get his claws out of you unless we deliver him the real murderer wrapped up in a giant bow."

"Janice Teller," Julia murmured into the rim of her mug. She was the only person Julia could think of with the opportunity and a motive.

"We need to find a way to make her talk," Sally said.

Julia nodded her agreement, but she was blown if she knew how. The wretched woman not only seemed to have gotten away from the scene of the crime without being seen, but now she'd found some other sap to pin it on. Namely her.

Sally sighed and gave Julia's arm a reassuring squeeze. "I've got to get down to the pub soon. I'm working this afternoon. You should come too, I don't like to think of you sitting here all alone."

"I'd have Rumpkin," Julia said.

"You know what I mean. Rumpkin's lovely but as conversationalist he's a bit lacking."

Julia would have preferred to pull a blanket over her head and disappear but she didn't have the strength to argue. "Fine, I'll come," she muttered.

* * *

Julia felt somewhat more human after the tea. She dressed in her warmest jumper and coat and managed to find a pair of jeans that was loose-fitting enough that she couldn't see the line of the ankle tag when she inspected herself in the full-length mirror in Sally's bedroom.

She had let Sally go on ahead of her. She hadn't wanted to hold Sally up and make her late for her shift, for one thing. She also quite wanted the time on her own to reflect. But once she was actually alone with her thoughts, she just found herself going around in mental circles.

Janice had the opportunity to kill Mrs White. Providing she was canny about it. Lift the keys on the way into the pub, then during the meal sneak out the back exit by the loos. Do the deed and hurry back. It certainly seemed like she'd been missing for a good chunk of time during the meal, according to the diners Julia had talked to. Although with the blue-rinse brigade, half of them didn't know where they'd last parked their dentures either, so she took their information with a pinch of salt.

And motive? Janice had that in spades. Surely someone needed a powerful, deep-seated motive to drive them to murder, especially in a tiny village like Biddle Rhyne where the inhabitants didn't exactly have a propensity for violence. Even on a Saturday night at the Fox and Hounds it was rare that anyone would raise their voice in anger let alone their fist.

With her mind lost in these thoughts, Julia left the house and began the walk towards the pub. As she entered the alleyway between the garden fences, she caught a strand of hair on the overhanging brambles and gave a tiny gasp of pain as it tore free. Rubbing the side of her head, she came out onto the country lane.

And then suddenly there she was.

Mrs Teller stood with her elbows resting on the top of a metal five-bar gate, looking out over the fields towards the looming shape of Pagan's Hill, the chill wind sweeping in off the moors and blowing her hair about her.

Julia took a deep breath. Now that she had the opportunity, she felt a sudden urge to just tuck her head down and carry on to the warmth and the comfort of the Barley Mow. If nothing else, she could come back with Sally.

But, no, she'd spent too long trying and failing to talk with Janice and she couldn't risk letting the woman slip through her fingers now. She walked up and planted herself next to Janice, doing her best to stand tall and keep the tremor out of her voice.

"I need to talk to you," she said.

Janice didn't look over, or acknowledge her in any way, she just kept gazing out over the sodden fields. The wind picked up again in another gust and her sandy blonde hair flew in streamers about her face.

Julia studied her, unsure what to do when presented with this absolute level of stonewalling, but eventually Janice broke her silence.

"I know why you're here," she said, her voice sounded level and drained of all emotion.

Julia suspected that she, too, had been crying not long before and was now in the wake of that surge of emotion that left you feeling wan and stretched out.

Janice continued, still looking out across the moor. "I'm tired of pretending. What's the point? It's so exhausting, isn't it? So let's not play games anymore. Not me, at least. I did it. Is that what you wanted from me?"

At long last Janice turned her head to face Julia, her crystal-blue eyes so intense that Julia could hardly bear to meet them. A single tear ran down Janice's face and she lifted a finger to quickly swipe it away.

Julia let out her breath long and slow. She could feel her heartbeat increasing. *A confession.* What should she do? Try and tape it? Call the police? She glanced about for a passer-by who could be an impartial witness in case Janice's attack of conscience passed over, but they were completely alone.

"Yes, I did it," Janice repeated. "I had a fumble with that clod of a waiter in your pub toilets during the meal."

Julia's mind worked rapidly to try and fit the pieces together. It didn't seem to make sense but the word 'clod' slid neatly into place.

"Do you mean Barry?" she asked.

Janice's shoulders gave the faintest tremble as she shrugged. "He's your boyfriend, I assume. I'm sorry."

"No, he's not," Julia answered quickly. The very thought of her and Barry intimately together made her feel a bit queasy. Quickly and unbidden it was followed by images of Barry and Janice together in the rather tight confines of the Barley Mow's toilets and bile rose in her throat.

Janice let out a long, heavy sigh and she pulled a cigarette from her handbag. "You don't mind, do you?"

Julia said she didn't, but Janice's trembling hand was already cupping the lighter to it before she'd answered. She inhaled deeply on the smoke. "I suppose Lance will find out soon enough. He'll be so angry."

"Even after..." Julia began before she could stop herself, but trailed off when she realized the bee's nest that she was about to put her verbal foot into.

"Yes, dear. Even after the affair he carried on for all those years," Janice replied. She shook her head. Even stressed and crying, Julia couldn't help thinking how beautiful she was. She could surely have had any man that she chose and here was where she'd ended up. A philanderer of a husband and a slovenly pub waiter.

Janice blew out some smoke and watched it curl into nothingness. "And I'd been faithful all this time, too. What bad timing I had for my little fling. Oh. I shouldn't have said that. A woman is dead, I shouldn't be so callous."

"What are you going to do now?" Julia asked.

Janice stared ahead again for a spell as a heron made its ponderous way over the field, following the path of one of the rhynes. "I don't know. I've never been one for planning ahead."

"Why don't you come with me to the Barley Mow?" Julia said. "Misery loves company."

Janice shifted leaning against the top of the gate with one arm so that she was now facing Julia. She seemed to be scrutinizing her from head to toe. Julia found it surprisingly difficult to stand still under the inspection. "You're miserable?" Janice asked finally.

Julia gave a little nod. For some reason she couldn't face putting the truth into words. Not even for a relative stranger like Janice Teller. "I've just been fired from Donaldson's." That seemed easier to process than being arrested. More real.

"And you enjoyed working at Donaldson's did you? It always struck me as a rather dingy place. Lacking soul."

"I need the money," Julia replied.

"Ah, yes. Of course. Don't listen to me, I don't know why I'm handing out advice. You'll end up living in a draughty cottage somewhere, besotted with a temperamental potter who considers himself an artist."

"A policeman's son in my case," Julia muttered, unable to help herself.

"Even worse."

Julia let out a sharp laugh and to her surprise found that Janice was laughing, too.

Janice stood stiffly and stretched out her back. "No. Thanks for the offer but I'll go home, such as it is, and face the music. As for you, you're young and resourceful. You'll think of something, mark my words."

With that, Janice began to walk slowly along the lane in the direction of Pagan's Hill and her unhappy cottage.

Julia watched her until the long sweep of the lane took her out of sight, and then she turned and headed in the other direction.

She believed Janice's story, but it didn't change anything. Someone had still stitched her up. But that person didn't have a face now, so there was no one to target her anger towards and the anger drifted away from her instead, leaving her feeling wooden and empty. At least when she had thought Janice had murdered Mrs White she had some hope of clearing her own name, but now? She sniffed and did her best to hold back tears. It was all so very hopeless.

Julia was lost in these bleak thoughts when she found herself at the Barley Mow, its sign swinging gently overhead in the wind. She crunched her way over the gravel car park and pulled the latch up on the door to the parlour.

It wasn't busy. Hardly surprising for a weeknight. The major was there, tucked away in his usual seat with the log fire crackling away next to him, reading his paper but looking like he was about to doze off, as he often did. Sally was behind the bar in her black uniform, in the middle of pulling a drink for a customer.

But something seemed off. Sally pulled a face at Julia as she entered. Although she couldn't fathom what it meant.

When the man at the bar turned around she realized what Sally was trying to say.

It was Lance Teller. His broad frame looked presentable enough in the striped, button-down shirt, but even from the brief moment of him turning, Julia could tell from the way Lance moved that he was blind drunk.

Clutching a pint of bitter in one hand, he staggered forward, nearly half the contents sloshing over the edge and onto the flags as he did so. He took one more step and his head collided noisily with the black wood of one of the low beams. He cried out and rubbed furiously at his forehead, but Julia could see there was more to his pain than just the bump to his head. His colour was rising and she saw tears appearing in his eyes.

"I know you all hated her!" he bellowed, throwing his arms out wide and depositing even more of his drink onto the floor.

In the corner, the major snorted and sat upright, suddenly awake. It wasn't clear who Lance was talking to, he seemed to be addressing the room or even the world in general.

"I know you all hated her. But Audrey was a wonderful woman. She was kind. And hard-working. And clever. She made something of her life, which is more than any of you can say. And she loved me. And I loved her!"

He lurched forward and grabbed Julia by the shoulder with his free hand, holding onto her so hard that it hurt. She tried to shy away but his grip was too strong. His face was inches from hers, tears leaking down his cheeks now. When he spoke she could smell the alcohol strong on his breath.

"There! You wanted to know if we had an affair. Well, we did. We were in love. I was going to leave Janice. Leave my wife of seven years. But she's gone now. A senseless, senseless tragedy." At the end of his speech he trailed off with a whimper.

Julia tried again to edge away but he was holding firm, his hand shaking with pent-up anger.

Somewhere in this commotion, Ivan had appeared at the door through to the eating area. He moved his large body through into the parlour and laid a hand gently on Lance's back. "Come on, pal, it's time to go, I think."

Lance gave out a very long sigh and let his own hand slip from Julia's shoulder, his fingertips trailing along the sleeve of her coat. "I wish we could have had that one final day," he said in a hushed voice. "I'd planned to tell her that day; that I'd leave Janice. If only she had made it. It would have meant the world to her to know that I'd chosen her. It would have. But she never made it." At that point his face broke and he began to sob.

Ivan had collected the man's coat from the peg and he draped it over Lance's shoulders even as he ushered him out of the pub's door with practised movements. The two men disappeared from sight as the door swung back behind them, but through the thin wood Julia could still hear the muffled sounds of Lance sobbing and the milder tones of Ivan's inaudible words as he tried to comfort him.

Julia stared around, barely believing what had just happened. The major returned her stare, wide-eyed, but instantly began sinking back down into a slouch, his head nodding so that his moustache almost dangled in the foam of his bitter.

Julia staggered over and almost collapsed across the bar, letting out a low whistle. "Poor Lance," she said.

"Poor Lance?" Sally echoed.

Julia nodded. "Maybe we were too harsh when we turned the screw on him the other day. He's obviously grieving."

"He was cheating on his wife," Sally practically spat. "I can't say I've much sympathy for him, the snake."

"But still," Julia said. "He obviously loved Mrs White."

"I can't see how." Sally crossed her arms. She saw that she wasn't going to convince her friend and shook her head. "Let's get you a drink. Wine? Or something a bit stronger?"

The major's voice piped up by Julia's shoulder making her jump. "Maybe you could just pour mine while the lady's deciding?" he said to Sally, plonking his empty glass down onto the top of the bar as he spoke.

In spite of it all, Julia couldn't help but marvel. That glass had been full not thirty seconds before.

Once Sally had handed him his drink, the major retreated back to his table and loud nasal snores were soon emanating from his corner.

Julia pulled up a stool and settled in. With the major asleep, the two women had the parlour to themselves. It was almost like old times. Until Julia's phone alarm sounded to remind her that she had to leave for her curfew.

Chapter 18

Julia made her way back down the pavement-less country lane by the light off her phone torch. It was still only about half seven but the evenings were coming in fast at this time of year.

Despite the bleakness of the walk she had so many fond memories of coming this way with Sally and her other school friends that it seemed somehow unbelievable that she could have such serious worries on her mind now.

In the distance, she could hear the loud rev of a car engine breaking the quiet of the evening. Someone evidently had places to be.

Something about what Lance had said in the pub was bothering her. He said he'd been going to tell Mrs White that he'd leave his wife, but he'd not gotten the chance because on the day that she was killed Mrs White had never shown up at his cottage.

She stopped dead in her tracks.

If that was true, then Mrs White hadn't been run down on her way back from her liaison with Lance, she had been run down on her way to it.

Julia shook her head and continued on her journey.

If that was the case then her whole timeline was wrong. All those alibis she had meticulously rooted out or poked holes in and Mrs White had already been lying dead for two hours.

She had so many thoughts jostling for attention in her mind that it made her head hurt. Think through this logically, she told herself.

So who could have taken the major's car keys two hours earlier? That would put it a little before ten o'clock.

No, wait. The pub wouldn't have been open at ten. How could the major have driven down if someone had already stolen the keys from his pocket?

Her mouth went dry and Julia cursed herself for her stupidity. It all fitted together neatly now.

The major had run Mrs White down as she was crossing Forge's Lane to go and meet Lance, as she did every Sunday. And then he had got out of the car, tossed the keys away somewhere and just sauntered down the hill at his own pace and walked through the front door of the pub.

And then he sat there drinking his usual pint of bitter and reading his newspaper like nothing had happened.

His whole plan had almost come a cropper because Julia was filling in the shift at the bar. He'd made a point to draw attention to himself when getting his second drink, knowing that Ivan would ask for his keys.

Then the major further made a point of looking for his keys and then his car, declaring it stolen and setting a timeline for when the car was taken and by extension when Mrs White was killed. The only person who might realize the timeline was wrong was Lance. But since he thought it was a senseless hit-and-run, the major knew he was unlikely to think much about whether the accident happened before or after their tryst, not realizing how crucial the timing was. And certainly the major didn't think he would go around discussing it, having kept schtum about the affair for years.

The major just hadn't counted on the man having a skinful and baring his heart. Like everyone else, he'd just assumed Lance was carrying on the affair in order to get his pots stocked at the garden centre at a bumper rate.

Lost in this train of thought, Julia had almost made it back to the alleyway leading to the residential streets.

Behind her, the engine noise grew louder and louder and bright headlights approached, casting Julia's long, distorted shadow in front of her, dancing with the vehicle's movement.

Julia turned, holding her arm up in front of her face to shield her eyes from the glare of the headlights. The car was still thundering up the lane and showing no sign of stopping. She edged to the reeds at the side of the road but the car didn't budge over an inch. Julia froze. For a moment, she thought the car was going to hit her, sending her the way of Mrs White.

But at the last second the car swerved, its tyres squealing on the asphalt, and then came to a screeching halt, the vehicle turned sideways across the road, blocking her off from the village.

The driver's door opened and the major stepped out, straightening up to his full height, his face pallid and ghoulish in the dim, shaky light of Julia's phone torch. His face was quite impassive but Julia could see the glint of malice in his eyes. She had no desire to wait and find out what he was capable of.

She turned around. It was dark in front of her. The Barley Mow out of sight around the corner and seemed an incredibly long way away now. The feeble light of her torch revealed almost nothing of the deserted country lane. All the same she started off at a run into the darkness.

She hadn't made it more than a few paces when a deep voice rang out from behind her.

"Now, you stop, Julia, or I'll shoot."

Julia came to a teetering halt, panting heavily. It might be a bluff, but she wasn't going to take that chance. She took a deep breath, trying to stop her hands from shaking with fear, and made herself slowly turn around to face her attacker.

The major stood a few paces from his car, seeming quite relaxed and still. In his right hand he was holding a little black gun, casually pointed in Julia's direction. He twitched the barrel, indicating back the way they'd come. "Right, come on, my girl, into the car."

Julia could feel her heart beating faster than it ever had before, but she felt rooted to the tarmac. "Why?" she managed to gasp.

She had meant it in a broader sense. 'Why kill Mrs White?' 'Why are you doing this to me?' But the major fielded the question rather literally.

"Well, I can't run another ruddy woman over with my car, can I?" he said. "Even the unenviable mind of Detective Inspector Jones would become suspicious if two of my vehicles ended up with bodies underneath them in as many weeks."

Julia blinked as she took this in. So she had been correct that the major had killed Mrs White then. That would be some consolation, now she could die happy as the serial killer made her his next victim.

The major twitched the gun again. "Come on, into the car."

Obviously nothing good was going to come from getting into that car. But the major could shoot her right there and then and leave her body lying in the rhyne. Every moment she could spin this out for was another moment when she might think of something.

With a shudder, Julia made her way along the lane, her feet feeling like lumps of concrete. She instinctively tried to keep as much space as she could between her and the major as she passed him. He pivoted slowly around to keep the gun trained on her.

"Drop the torch," he said.

Julia hesitated. The major prodded her in the small of the back with the pistol and she jumped into the air with a squeal.

"Hush," the major growled. "Drop the torch."

Julia's hand was shaking so hard she found it difficult to let go, eventually managing to will her fingers apart. The phone fell with a clatter onto the verge, the light lost in the long grass.

"Now, into the car," the major instructed.

She carried on, aware of the major trailing along close behind. When they reached the car the major pressed a button in his key fob and the boot made a clicking sound and popped ajar. "In," he said.

Julia peered through the crack in the door at the tiny confines within. "Please," she said, turning around to face the major. "Not the boot. I won't try anything, I swear."

The major's face remained unmoved. "In," he repeated.

Julia tried to make her muscles move but she couldn't face the grim fate of climbing into the back of that car. The major extended his hand, bringing the gun level with her head, only a few inches from the side of her face. "I won't say it again," he said.

Just then there was the sound of a car further up the road in the direction of the Barley Mow, a high-pitched groan echoing over the fields as the engine fought for power. Julia and the major looked around at the sound and saw a pair of headlights racing down the lane.

Julia's heart rose, the cavalry, whoever it was, was here and just in the nick of time. The major recoiled slightly and drew his arm down but kept the gun trained on Julia.

The car swerved and came to a dramatic halt, skidding the last few feet along the road, jerking to a stop just in front of them, the full beams causing them both to squint.

The car sat purring for a few moments and then the headlights dimmed and from the plain, grey sedan the form of DI Jones hauled himself out, using one hand on the roof of the car for purchase, and strode purposefully towards them. As he marched, he reached around to the back of his hip and produced a pair of handcuffs, glinting in the light of his car headlamps. He tossed them gently up and down, as though getting the weight of them.

"Caught right in the act!" Jones declared gleefully as he huffed and puffed his way towards them, the major retreating another step.

"Turn around please, Miss Ford," the inspector said, addressing Julia.

"What? Why?" Julia asked.

"Don't play dumb, girl. You're out after curfew. I told you that you'd slip up, I just didn't realize that it would be this bloody soon. Honestly, we need a better calibre of criminal today."

Julia stared at Jones in disbelief, her jaw dropping. "The major has a gun," she said, loudly, enunciating each word carefully like she would speak to a Spanish waiter. "He was going to kill me."

The inspector's eyes swivelled around, apparently noticing the major and his weapon for the first time.

The major raised the gun again, training it on the inspector this time. "Back off, Jones, or I'll shoot."

Jones leaned in slightly and squinted at the gun. "It's fake," he said.

"It ruddy isn't," the major said.

"It ruddy is."

With that, Jones reached out with a flabby hand and plucked the little black pistol from the major's grasp, who seemed to offer only token resistance.

The major snorted with anger, the discharge from his nostrils ruffling his moustache on the way out. He balled his left hand into a fist and swung it in a wild haymaker arc, catching Jones completely by surprise and landing the blow heavily on the other man's cheek.

Jones staggered backwards, dropping the fake gun to the floor and bringing his hand up to his face. "Ow," he said, rubbing rigorously at the spot where the punch had landed.

"Plenty more where that came from," the major said, raising his fists about his head.

"Oh, I don't think so," the inspector said and he launched his large frame forward, arms swinging in from the sides to envelop his quarry.

Julia was reminded of a panther leaping to catch its prey. Only he was much wider, and lacked any of the natural grace and poise of a big cat. With his jacket billowing out behind, maybe he was more like a flying squirrel. A very large, heavy one.

It was surprisingly effective, though. Jones collided with the major and they both went down to the pavement in a tangled heap, the copper's arms wrapping the major up as they descended. There was a brief struggle on the ground as the major kicked and squirmed, but he was firmly lodged underneath Jones and the inspector showed no signs of budging.

Jones glanced up from the ground. "Ford, would you be so kind as to pass me the handcuffs?" he asked.

Julia looked down to where the cuffs lay, presumably dropped as the inspector had launched his tackle. "With pleasure, Inspector," she peeped and trotted over to hand them to him.

With a few deft moves, Jones managed to force the major's hands behind his back and Julia heard the satisfying clink of the cuffs snapping shut. It was a much nicer sound when it wasn't happening to her wrists, she decided.

Jones rose to his feet, hauling the major up as he did so. The major was turning a deep scarlet colour and trying unsuccessfully to blow bits of dirt from his moustache which had been lodged there during the scuffle.

Jones made a move towards his car but Julia stopped them.

"I still don't understand, Major," she said. "Why did you kill Mrs White?"

"I have my reasons!" the major spat. "Good ones, too."

Then it all suddenly dawned on Julia and she clapped her hands to her cheeks like a Munch painting. "You don't, do you? You have really, really petty reasons. You tiny little man."

The major huffed at her but didn't reply. Jones turned a quizzical face to her. "What are you thinking there, Ford?"

"It was the blasted garden centre expansion," she said. "Mrs White wanted to expand it and put some new buildings up. The council had approved it and the public consultation would have been little more than a formality."

"And what was wrong with this expansion?" Jones asked. He was talking to the major but Julia answered for him.

"It would spoil the view from his garden," Julia said.

Jones shook his head slowly. "I've seen some pretty vile things done for some daft reasons before. But this one might just take the cake," he said. "That explains the 'why', but what about the 'how'?"

Julia allowed herself a wry smile. "That's a long story, Inspector. But I can explain."

"Let's talk as we drive," Jones said.

With that, Jones gave the major a steady push between the shoulder blades and guided him into the back of his car.

Chapter 19

The Christmas lights twinkled away in the window, fading slowly in and out in their neat lines. It was still only November and normally Sally would have absolutely forbidden Julia from bringing the holiday decorations out before Advent. But, presumably sensing that her friend had needed some cheering up, Sally had actually been the one to suggest it, and so, earlier that afternoon, the two of them had braved the rickety fold-out steps to the loft which the landlord had promised to fix years ago, and hauled down the overstuffed cardboard box. Still, Sally had drawn the line at the lights and not allowed anything else to emerge from the box, claiming that she still had standards to maintain.

It was dark on the other side of the window and freezing rain had been drumming against the outside of the house since lunchtime. To Rumpkin's delight, Julia had ratcheted the gas fire up to its highest temperature because despite the cold weather she needed to wear her shorts. Her little white shorts that showed off all of her legs and most importantly her ankles. Her free, unencumbered, untagged ankles.

They were currently stretched out before Julia on a footstool, enjoying the gentle waves of warmth that flowed out of the fire, over the snoring dog and across to the armchair. Julia turned a page in her book, thankful that all the charges against her had been dropped and that she could happily shut the world out knowing that it was not going to bother her anymore.

A bottle of cabernet sat on the side table next to her, calling its siren song. Julia thought for a moment whether it was acceptable to have a third glass before teatime and concluded that was exactly what being a free woman was all about.

Her hand was just reaching towards the bottle when the chimes of the doorbell sounded throughout the house, sending Rumpkin yipping towards the front door.

"Don't worry, chicken, I'll get it," Julia heard Sally call from behind her and a smell of something delicious and cinnamony drifted out as the kitchen door opened.

Good old Sally. She had been firmly turning away local journalists all day. This sounded like something different, though, there was a hubbub of voices at the door, all talking over each other, with Rumpkin adding his occasional contribution, too. Julia risked turning in her chair and peeking over the top of it. Mark and both his mum and dad were in the doorway. Sally's body language was more open and welcoming than it had been with the assorted journalists and nosey parkers.

"Yes, she's just in the living room, come on through." Julia heard Sally's voice rising above the rest.

She cursed quietly. She was in her little shorts and her pyjama top, she really hadn't been counting on seeing anyone; Sally was meant to have seen to that.

Julia picked her book up off the arm of the chair. Normally having a book in hand would have lent her an air of sophistication, even in her current state of disrobement. But all her brain mush had been capable of after recent events was a pulpy bodice-ripper, so Julia flipped it coverside down instead.

She rose to try and get across to the bookshelves and snatch up something more cerebral, but she was too late. The family Jones trooped in from the hallway accompanied by a gust of chill air from outside, peeling their outer coats off as they came.

"Hello, Julia." There was a chorus from the visitors and Julia fluttered an arm up in a wave to reply.

After that, everyone stood around in a loose circle shuffling awkwardly and not knowing quite how to begin. Julia looked over to Mark but he gave a half-hearted smile and failed to meet her eye.

"Well," Sally said, breaking the silence and clapping her hands together. She was wearing a flour-covered apron that read 'No Sugar Thanks, I'm Sweet Enough Already'. "I'd better get back to my cinnamon buns or they'll burn. Shall I make some tea while I'm in the kitchen anyway?"

There was a general murmuring of assent and then Sally deftly exited the room, leaving Julia alone with the Joneses.

Mark's mum gave Julia a broad grin and at the same time elbowed her husband in the back of the ribs. "Go on," she hissed through clenched teeth.

The inspector shuffled half a step forward. He had hung his coat over the banister and now he was ringing his woolly Oddballs hat between his hands, as though doffing his cap to the local nobility. He cleared his throat, which apparently took some time. "Well, Miss Ford, I mean, Julia, I just wanted to say that, erm, everyone at the station was very impressed, and I should also say very grateful, with your, erm, help in apprehending Major Portland. So, yes, I just wanted to say thank you."

"You should be saying sorry for arresting her!" Sally's voice belted from the doorway.

Julia looked at her with a face of thunder and Sally disappeared back into the kitchen.

The inspector's moustache twitched. "Well, quite, yes. I also wanted to, you know, offer my apologies for the whole misunderstanding and having-you-arrested thing," he said.

"And tagged." Sally's voice came floating from the kitchen.

"Yes. And sorry for having you tagged."

Julia couldn't help but be moved by the overt display of contrition before her. "That's okay," she said softly. She almost meant it.

The inspector continued. "Although, thinking about it, if I hadn't tagged you, then I wouldn't have been able to come to your aid when…" He trailed off as he noticed the glare from his family members on either side of him.

"Which wouldn't have been necessary if you'd worked out what the major was up to beforehand," his wife reminded him gently, all the time her smile fixed on her face.

"Um, quite. Oh, and you were quite right about the iPad. When the IT boffins looked at it, they found the minutes for Mrs White's meeting with Mr Teller had been filled in in advance. I suppose it left more time for…" The inspector's eyes darted from his wife on one side to his son on the other and his face began to redden. Finally he finished weakly with, "…for other things."

DI Jones relinquished his grip on his hat in order to extend one of his large hands towards Julia, and after the briefest of hesitations she reached out and shook it.

Now it was Mark's turn to go through an extended throat-clearing routine. His mother looked at him and then placed a hand lightly on her husband's shoulder. "Perhaps we should go and see if that nice young woman needs a hand in the kitchen," she said.

The inspector gave her a quizzical look. "Why would she need our help?" he asked, but allowed himself to be ushered out of the room by his wife's repeated pats on the back.

Mrs Jones gave her son a slightly harassed look before beginning to follow her husband from the room. She paused by the armchair, picked up Julia's copy of *I Was Ravaged by a Polish Sea Captain*, raised her eyebrows and placed it carefully back on the chair before finally, mercifully, heading into the kitchen.

Mark watched her go and then turned to Julia, still unable to meet her eye. "I suppose I owe you an apology, too," he said.

It was funny to see him like this. So very meek and downbeat, when normally he was full to the brim with a cheeky energy.

"No, no." Julia waved her hands at him. "Don't be silly. With the magazine and everything, what else would you think? No apology needed from you."

"Yes, there is," Mark insisted. "I should have given you the benefit of the doubt. Or at least given you a chance to explain. Instead of siccing my dad on you."

"At least he came through in the end," Julia said, unsure why she was fighting Mark's corner for him. The way he'd acted towards her, she should have let him twist in the wind. But somehow her heart wasn't in it.

"I've heard about three dozen times the story of how he tackled the major to the ground," Mark said.

Julia couldn't help but smile. "It was rather something to see."

"All those Saturday morning tackling practices finally paying off then. I can't recall it ever helping him much on the pitch."

"I'm glad you've come anyway," Julia said, changing the subject. "I was worried that I'd seen the last of you."

And finally there was that signature grin that she'd come to know so very well. "We both know that wouldn't have happened. Not with baking like that going on in the house." He gestured towards the kitchen where admittedly extremely appetizing smells were wafting in from.

All the same, Julia gave him a gentle slap on the chest with the back of her hand for good measure. "You tease," Julia said.

Without warning, Mark bent down and gave Julia a quick peck on the lips.

In spite of herself, Julia felt a blush rising.

"Listen, Julia," Mark began. To her surprise he suddenly seemed a little anxious again, the self-assurance of the previous exchange rapidly melting away. "I know that it wasn't all that long ago that we met. But I think you're a really remarkable young woman, I honestly do. So, I had something that I wanted to ask you."

Epilogue

Julia closed her eyes and savoured the sound of church bells ringing out.

Mark's proposal had taken her completely by surprise and most of December had passed in a whirlwind of activity and relentless organization via spreadsheet.

His idea to open a bookshop made sense, though. She opened her eyes and bustled on down the high street, there was really no time to rest. Everyone she passed was bundled up tightly in scarves and hats against the cold weather. She was faintly regretting wearing her thickest coat, though. She'd been running hither and thither so much that she was sweating buckets underneath.

She stopped outside the library – no, she corrected herself – she stopped outside her shop. She corrected herself again – *their* shop. Mark had been the one to stump up two months' worth of lease money. And thrown himself whole hog into renovating the place and kitting it out as a shop. His van had been an almost permanent feature for the last two weeks; now it was parked there as usual, higgledy-piggledy on the pavement causing an obstacle for passers-by. She squeezed past it now to reach the glass double doors, a handmade 'Opening Soon' banner stuck diagonally across the nearest.

And what was she providing to the enterprise? She asked herself this for possibly the hundredth time. A name. A story to draw footfall in. She hadn't been convinced at first, but it did seem that her part in solving Mrs White's murder had made a ripple in the local news. A ripple that Mark was determined to ride as far as it would take them.

Julia had agreed to do every newspaper and local TV interview that had come her way, in exchange for the money and work that Mark had committed. She hadn't relished the glare of the spotlight, even if that spotlight didn't get any larger than the relative minnow that was *South West Regional News*. But seeing the bookshop taking shape in the old library had definitely made the discomfort worthwhile. She looked now at the outside of the building, trying to imagine it when it was finished. Instead of the pots of paint and stepladder in the window, they'd agreed to have a big True Crime display, using her minor celebrity status to maximum effect.

"Hello, Julia." A voice by her shoulder startled her out of her daydreams.

It was Barry, in his big puffy jacket with a stripy hat with earflaps pulled down far over his head.

"How's the work coming along?" he asked, pointing a mitten at the shop.

Julia smiled. "It's coming along. There's plenty to do, though. Especially if we want to be open on schedule." She mentally shuddered, thinking of the money flushed down the loo if they didn't manage to open their doors soon.

The support and well-wishes she'd been given for the shop had really warmed Julia's heart. Everyone in the village had been thrilled by the idea of a bookshop opening. Well, almost everyone. Mr Smedley had appeared a few days earlier and grilled them over which local authors they were going to be stocking. Apparently he'd been phoning around anyone stocked at the garden centre and tried to lock them into exclusive deals. Not many takers, though. At least, that was what Sally had told her, keeping her ear to the ground behind the bar.

"Not looking for any extra help, are you?" Barry asked.

"What about the Barley Mow?" Julia said.

Underneath his layers, Barry gave a shrug. "Ivan's a difficult man to work for. He keeps threatening to give me the can. I'm not sure how long I can stick it out there."

Julia gave him what she hoped was a reassuring smile. "Ivan talks a big game but he's actually a big softie. He's not firing anyone." She certainly hoped that was true. If things went as well as they'd cautiously thought it might, then they would need extra help and she didn't think she could face the idea of employing Barry.

"Well, I hope you're right. I'd better get on, I'm already late," Barry said, and with a brief nod he began to slowly sidle down the high street in the direction of the Barley Mow; Julia flattened herself against the side of Mark's van to let him squeeze by.

Julia watched him go and shook her head to herself. The lunch shift would already have started twenty minutes ago and he showed no signs of hurrying. She was just wondering how he managed to drift through life that way when she remembered that she'd promised Mark she'd only be gone a quarter of an hour, and pushed the front door open.

If Mark had noticed how long she'd been gone then he didn't show it. He looked up from his makeshift saw-horse formed by a couple of stepladders and smiled cheerily.

The shop had been a frenetic hive of activity, but most of that had been ripping out fixtures from the library they couldn't use or didn't want. Gone were the ancient, dented metal shelves. Gone were the overhead fluorescent lights, along with the dizzying volume of insects which had expired in them. Gone was the mildew-encrusted counter, and Mark was busy cutting the wood for its replacement.

Although it was progress, the result was scarred walls, sawdust covering the floor and gaping holes in the ceiling with half-wired spotlights hanging forlornly from them. It was looking pretty dire to Julia, but Mark's friend had assured them he'd be back later in the week to get them finished. Mark had called in an impressive number of favours and created an even greater number in order to get various friends, relatives and acquaintances to chip in with the seemingly unending list of tasks the construction project required.

Mark straightened up and placed the saw down, resting against one of the paint-speckled stepladders. "What did the vicar say?" he asked.

"He said that while he didn't feel it fully appropriate to do a sermon on the spiritual nature of a good book, he did fully endorse the shop and would make sure he came along on opening day."

"That's something at least," Mark said. "Get that chap on board and the congregation will be following, I'm sure."

"He did also say that he had a large stack of second-hand Christian books that he'd donate to the store."

Mark stretched, working out a tight knot in his shoulder. "I'm sure they'll just fly off the shelves," he said. "Now come on, you've had enough gadding about. Grab a wood plane; there's work to be done."

Julia picked the plane up from the oversized toolbox which had taken up residency in the centre of the room, and set to work.

There was something therapeutic and calming in the repetitive motions, and seeing the wood shaped before her. She was looking forward to the village returning to its normal, sedate pace of life, safe in the knowledge that it would be a long, long time before a sleepy little place like Biddle Rhyne would see another murder in its midst.

She had no idea just how wrong she was.

Acknowledgements

I'd like to thank my wonderful writing group: JP Weaver, Kendall Olsen-Maier, MachineCapybara, Caitlin L. Strauss and Delilah Waan. I've learnt a lot from all of you.

I'd also like to thank my wife, for never once objecting when I disappear to write, and to my mum and dad for their help refining the later stages of the book, especially Mum for her efforts in proofreading.

Finally I'd like to thank Marianna, Erik, Polly, Tarek and Annaliza at The Book Folks for their hard work, and their incredible patience.

If you enjoyed this book, please let others know by leaving a quick review on Amazon. Also, if you spot anything untoward in the paperback, get in touch. We strive for the best quality and appreciate reader feedback.

editor@thebookfolks.com

www.thebookfolks.com

More fiction in this series

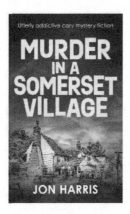

Released late October 2023

Julia has accomplished her dream of opening a bookshop!
Well, almost. It still needs refurbishing, and there are some
tricky planning laws to get around. But small beer! Yet she
is stopped in her tracks when tragedy strikes once more.
Someone is digging up the past in Biddle Rhyne, and
sticking knives into people's backs. Quite literally,
unfortunately…

Other titles of interest

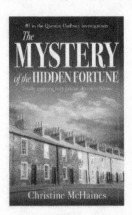

THE MYSTERY OF THE HIDDEN FORTUNE
by Christine McHaines

Quentin Cadbury, a useless twenty-something, is left to look after his late aunt's London house when his parents head to Australia. But burglars seem determined to break in, and not even the stray cat he befriends can help him. As the thieves are after something pretty valuable, and illegal, he must grow up pretty fast to get out of a sticky situation.

FREE with Kindle Unlimited and available in paperback!

THE MISSING AMERICAN
by Julie Highmore

Private detective Edie Fox is more than a little suspicious
when a wealthy American turns up to her cluttered
backstreet office and hands her a bundle of cash to find
his missing cousin. But not enough to turn down the deal.
Yet she soon has more on her hands than she bargained
for when an old flame enters her life, and the witnesses in
her case start giving her the run-around.

FREE with Kindle Unlimited and available in paperback!

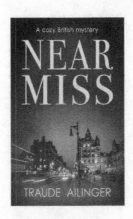

NEAR MISS
by Traude Ailinger

After being nearly hit by a car, fashion journalist Amy Thornton decides to visit the driver, who ends up in hospital after evading her. Curious about this strange man she becomes convinced she's unveiled a murder plot. But it won't be so easy to persuade Scottish detective DI Russell McCord.

FREE with Kindle Unlimited and available in paperback!